Hell's Kitties
And Other
Beastly Beasts

Edited by April Grey

Published by Lafcadio Press
New York City

Dedicated to the Dude.

Contents

Introduction
Hell's Kitties and Other Beastly Beasts

Welcome to Hell's Kitties and Other Beastly Beasts, the third book of the Hell's series. In these pages you'll meet ferocious felines, creepy canines and foul fowls.

This volume is dedicated to the Dude.

Let me tell you about the Dude...

On a warm night in October 2015, I received a call from one of my fellow community gardeners. Our community garden is right next to my building (and was the inspiration for Hell's Garden: Mad, Bad and Ghostly Gardeners). Heavy rain clouds hung in the sky about to open and my friend had left his notebook in the garden. Could I find it and leave it in the shed?

It was already dark, but the spill of light from neighboring buildings cast long, weird shadows through the foliage and tree limbs of the old garden. The pathways are uneven and can be dangerous, even in broad daylight. Several years back, I had broken my arm on the steps.

I undid the padlock on the gate and, guided by the flashlight on my smart phone, crept in. The sweet aroma of autumn clematis, shimmering white in the darkness, tickled my nose. Red and golden mums faintly glowed in the shadows cast by the light from my phone.

I put one step ahead of another, quite certain I'd trip if I looked away. Already a cooler breeze rustled the leaves on the path, heralding rain. I inched myself to the bench where my friend had left his notebook.

Nothing.

I phoned him. "It's not there."

"Try the back area."

Which meant going down the very steps that had broken my arm.

My breath hitched as I took the stairs. The darned notebook sat on the table by the shed.

"Found it," I said, quite pleased that I was still alive and in one piece. From the shrubs, two small, bright eyes glinted mysteriously in the periphery of the light from my phone. "I'm not alone."

"Hope it's not a rat." My friend was never good at reassurance.

The gleaming eyes moved closer, revealing its owner. "It's a kitten." I moved slowly, afraid of scaring it off.

"Okay, well, leave the notebook in the shed and I'll drop by tomorrow."

I put the book in the shed and wondered what I would do next. Sometimes we'd get cats in the garden, people left them there thinking… what, they'd live off of the rodents that we routinely poisoned? More likely the poor creature would run out into the road and get hit by a car, or drink antifreeze from puddles.

I couldn't leave the kitty. "Hey there." I leaned down. The kitten showed no fear, came right up to me for a head rub. It wore a collar. Then I knew I had to take it upstairs. Salem, our sixteen-year-old partially-sighted cat wouldn't like it, but I'd keep the kitten separate. I scooped it into my arms to inch myself back to the front of the garden. Amazing the feline didn't try to escape as I juggled it and the key to the padlock on the gate and then my front door.

My husband and son hooted in delight. We'd held off getting a second cat because of Salem's age and infirmity, but we had secretly longed for one. He was black like Salem, but Salem had mismatched eyes of brown and gold while our new friend had pure apple-green eyes. We named him the Dude because of his laid back personality.

Laid back? In the following days and weeks, we revised our opinion.

Nothing was safe from this purring ball of fluff, not the drapes, not the food in the cupboards, not our feet as they were pounced on with tiny, sharp claws. His mission seemed to be to turn our tranquil household upside down.

Reluctant, yet duty bound, I prowled the neighborhood with a picture of the Dude in his red collar, searching for the owner with no success. Eventually I had the vet check for a chip and found none. Having the Dude neutered meant he was ours for good, or so we thought.

Salem tolerated our new cat well; little fur flew, even though our Kitty from Hell constantly found new ways to raise Cain. The geraniums in a planter took a mortal hit from the Dude's incessant digging paws—maybe that was why he was in the garden? He took over our home, and our hearts, as he snuggled and frolicked with my husband, son and me.

One day when tulips and snowdrops again graced our garden, our son brought my attention to the Dude stretched out in our living room gasping for air. I recognized the symptoms from when our first Chihuahua went into cardiac arrest: the peculiar sound and movement as the lungs fill with fluid.

I ran him to the emergency vet, praying that I was wrong. So young, it couldn't be a heart problem, the vet would have told me.

The Dude crossed the Rainbow Bridge after a week of noble battle. A heart condition that he tried his best to rally against.

He left us that spring; only five short months since we met and fell in love, and we are still heart-broken. Though a sweet and loving fellow, the Dude was also Mischief in Fur.

So I'm dedicating this volume to the Dude.

Finally, half the authors in this anthology are British—I chose to retain the flavor of their native lands by not Americanizing their spelling and grammar. So if you come across color spelled as colour, it is not a typo

Thanks for picking up Hell's Kitties and do leave a review if you liked what you read.

April Grey, NYC September 2016

A Feline Familiar
By Rayne Hall

A magickal cat needs a forever home.

November wind rattles the windows and rain gusts against the panes. The cats have withdrawn to the kennel's heated indoor section and curled up in their cosy donut beds. Some doze with heads on paws, others watch my fingers dance across the keyboard, ears tilted forward as they listen to the rhythmic clack-clack-clack.

Several stare intently at the door, waiting.

They seem to know it's a Saturday, the day when the Feline Familiars sanctuary opens its doors, and potential adopters drop in, wizards in search of a magickal assistant and pet.

The first arrival, alas, has not come to adopt one of my charges. She places a cat carrier on the rickety table by the door, shakes the raindrops from her purple mane and juts her chin. "Ms Landen, this cat is no good."

My heart plummets: a reject. I remember the cat this young woman adopted three weeks ago. "I'm sorry to hear that. What's the problem with Hekate?"

"She's supposed to be a genuine magickal familiar." The customer points an index finger at the carrier and tosses her head so vigorously that her dyed tresses fly. "Are you intentionally misleading customers, Ms Landen? I tried her, and she has no magick. None whatsoever."

I click to open Hekate's computer file. A blue screen announces, "Word experienced an error trying to open the file." My old laptop is overdue for replacement, but the budget is stretched thin with vet's bills, huge amounts of cat food, and heating to keep this basement warm in winter.

My mind holds information on every animal in my care, so I don't need the computer's help to recall Hekate's details: nine-year-old female, came to the shelter four months ago, owner-surrender, micro-chipped, spayed. Her owner, an elderly witch, was ill and could no longer care for her companion. According to her, Hekate was "hugely intuitive with remarkable psychic gifts, a good conductor of magick."

The old lady probably exaggerated her beloved pet's abilities. I don't blame her for trying to secure her darling a good home, but it leaves me with a big problem.

I walk to the table by the door and give the purple-maned witch a pacifying smile. "Let's see, shall we?" I unzip the carrier's front flap, expecting to see a bewildered, distressed cat. Instead, Hekate strides out with the confident grace of a black panther. She rubs her head against my arm, then sits on the edge of the table, scanning the one-room shelter-shop-office like a queen surveying her realm.

I caress her black coat, soft and smooth like silk. It will be difficult to find a forever home for this old lady. Most magicians want young familiars they can train to their ways, not a senior in her sunset years. Especially not one without magic.

Stroking Hekate from the crown of her head to the tip of her tail, the way she likes it, I point my free hand at the kennel. "Would you like to see which of our cats resonates best with your magick?"

Eleven cats are waiting, all awake and alert now, pushing against the bars to get noticed. Some hold their tails upright in a 'come pick me' pose.

The young woman pulls at her layered capes and gives a nervous laugh. "Are you sure they're different?"

Suddenly I see what's going on. This girl with her purple hair, tie-dye skirts and crystal pendants - she has no magick. She sought a cat to compensate for her lack. Too lazy to put in the practice needed to master magick, she expected the cat to provide instant results. I can see her in my mind's eye, like a movie...

In a yellow haze, she dances on a round rug with pentagram pattern, skyclad but for a dozen occult pendants dangling on her chest, the paperback 1001 Instant Spells For The Teenage Witch in her hand.

If only I had perceived this at the screening interview three weeks ago! But I'm not particularly intuitive and definitely not psychic. I'm not even a good judge of character. When interviewing clients who want to adopt a cat, I just ask questions to see if they'll treat the animal with kindness and offer a suitable home.

I decide to put my impression to the test. "I'll open the kennel, so you can meet our current cats. Then I'll observe how they respond to your kind of magick, and recommend the right one."

Of course that's not something I could truly do. The magickal bond between human and feline emerges only after weeks of close interaction, trust and respect, not at a first encounter.

A flush creeps across the teenage witch's cheeks and she looks at her shoes. "I don't really have the time."

I'm right: she's frightened to expose her ignorance of magick.

"Maybe you want to come back another day when you have more time," I suggest tactfully. "I'll print you off a voucher which you can exchange for a cat any day in the future. Or you can spend it on something from our gift range." I gesture to the merchandise shelf with its displays of cat goddess statues, tumble stones and gemstone pendants.

She lets out a huge breath. "Yes, that will be good." She takes the empty carrier and waits for the voucher — which I have to scribble by hand, because the laptop won't power up — gathers her layered capes around her, and departs.

This still leaves me with the problem of Hekate.

If the old cat really has no affinity for magick, could I place her with another animal shelter? But the local places are overflowing, and their resources are stretched even thinner than mine. They struggle to provide for the animals already in their care, and are forced to euthanise those who don't get adopted fast.

Few people want to adopt a black cat. They adhere to superstitions that black cats bring bad luck or are minions of evil. Hekate's chances look bleak.

I stroke Hekate's silky coat along the length of her spine, and she purrs softly, grateful for the caress.

The door jingles, and another visitor arrives, a man with a firm stride and a friendly smile. Caradoc is a real magician and one of my favourite clients. Not only has he adopted several of our cats over the years, but he's helped me with magickal aid on occasion, protecting the sanctuary against vandals and driving away the rain clouds that threatened the fundraising bazaar. A little older than I, he's handsome with bright blue eyes, silver-streaked dark hair and strong hands with manicured nails.

"Blessed be, Lavinia," he greets. He gives me a smile that instantly brightens my day, and turns to Hekate who still sits on the table by the door. "Wow, this one has magick!"

If Caradoc says so, it's true. Unlike me, he can sense magickal powers in all creatures.

"She's just been returned as a reject," I tell him. "The client who brought her says she has no magick at all."

He raises his silver eyebrows. "That wannabe witch who just left? That figures."

Caradoc possesses the kind of insight into people that I wish I had. He only needs to look at someone for a few seconds to form a dependable judgement. I'm glad he likes me.

He reaches out to stroke Hekate. She backs away.

"She's skittish," I feel obliged to explain. "She's just been rejected and feels shy."

"I'll take her." He grabs to lift Hekate into his arms.

She squirms, hisses, rakes claws across his face.

"Feck!" He tosses her against the wall.

It's a powerful throw, and Hekate wails in pain. Then, as she cowers under the table, he steps closer and kicks her in the side. When he turns to me again, his lips curve in a tolerant smile. "She's a spirited girl

15

and will need some time to get used to me. But I'll take her."

My mind whirls. What has just happened? What does it mean?

Caradoc just hurt a cat before my eyes! But I've known him for years, he's a good man. Hekate scratched his face — he tossed her away from him in a reflex act, without meaning to. That kick, on the other hand... A sudden coldness hits me at the core. That kick was deliberate. He meant to hurt.

Huddled in the far corner under the table, well away from Caradoc's shined leather shoes, Hekate sends me a beseeching gaze from yellow eyes.

"You won't take her," I hear myself saying. Where did this resolution come from?

"What?" He gives me an incredulous stare. A moment later, his self-possession is back. "You're right, Lavinia. She clearly doesn't fancy me, and it's never good to take a female who doesn't care for you from her own free will. I'll choose another."

He walks along the kennel's edge, peering in. Many eager cats rub against the bars.

Hekate keeps staring at me, her gaze so hypnotic that my whole vision tints yellow. Suddenly I see an image of Caradoc working magick in a circle of green light. On the table before him lies a cat, strapped down. Now I hear the sounds of the scene, the cat's squeals of pain and fear. With every feline scream, magickal energy rises as green light, and gets absorbed by Caradoc.

Nausea churns my stomach and spirals into my throat. I try to blink away the vision, but Hekate wills me to understand.

I begin to comprehend. I'm not a psychic – but Hekate is. Her old witch had described her as 'hugely intuitive with remarkable psychic gifts'. She can see into Caradoc's soul, replay his memories and intentions... and she's transmitting them to me.

Dizzy and sick, I grab my mug and gulp down some tea to ground myself. As my rational reasoning returns, everything falls into place. Caradoc torments animals, feeding his magick with their pain. That's why he adopted eleven cats in two years.

I rise, clutching the desk for support. "It's best if you don't come here again."

A deep furrow draws on his brow, and he appears to stare right into my heart to probe if I really mean it. Then he shrugs and strides out. The door jingles and closes behind him with a thud.

What have I done?

I've lost the sanctuary a good customer and supporter – that's bad. But I've protected the cats in my care, and that's what counts.

Hekate relaxes. She hops onto my lap, rubs her head against my arm and purrs. I stroke her absent-mindedly while I take stock of the situation.

Without Caradoc's aid, the Feline Familiars sanctuary's resources will be even more tightly stretched, but we will manage. He might place a vengeful spell on us, but I think that's unlikely, and I can ask our other clients to create protective wards. Deprived of his supply of magickal felines, he may turn to ordinary cats, so I'll give the other shelters in the area a call to alert them about a suspected animal abuser.

What about Hekate, though?

"Mirr, mrrrr!" she says. She slides off my lap, crosses the room, and leaps onto the table by the entrance. Like a gatekeeper statue, she gazes at the door.

The message is clear: she intends to stay here, and vet the humans who come to adopt felines. She'll help me with the screening interviews. I'm neither psychic nor intuitive or even good at judging people – but Hekate excels. Together, we'll make the perfect team.

The door handle dips. Hekate's ears tilt forward.

"You got the job," I tell her. Then I shout, "Come right in, we're open."

Rayne Hall writes fantasy, horror and non-fiction. Her black cat Sulu – adopted from the rescue shelter - likes to snuggle between her arms while she writes, purring happily.

After living in Germany, China, Mongolia and Nepal, Rayne has settled in a seaside town in England. She enjoys reading, gardening and long walks along the seashore, braving ferocious seagulls and British rain.

She is the author of over sixty books, mostly dark fantasy and creepy horror, as well as the bestselling Writer's Craft series.

Visit her website raynehall.com, or follow her on Twitter https://twitter.com/RayneHall for writing tips and photos of her cute clever cat.

Territory
By Anya Davis

The wails of fighting cats are common sounds in the city after night has fallen – but what happens when a human intervenes?

Everything seems louder after dark. The churning of the diesel engine as I step down from the bus: the slap of my sandals on the pavement; the distant hollers of rowdier revellers making their way home from the city's bars and clubs. Each sound is amplified, incongruous with the stillness of the residential streets.

I pause in front of the railway arch that acts as the entrance to the alley. It's only the stench that puts me off, the putrid aroma emanating from the rotting rubbish that lines the walls and forms a festering mountain by the archway. The far end of the passage is visible, the street light emitting an inviting marmalade glow. My front door is just a few seconds' walk from there. All is quiet. This well-lit shortcut, overlooked by neighbouring houses, is more welcoming than the alternative route, the bustling main road lined with takeaways, where lecherous drunks lurch from doorways and scuffles break out between gangs of posturing lads with something to prove. That always seems like their territory to me.

I stride towards the street lamp, trying to put thoughts of the vermin that could be scampering through the filth to the back of my mind. I'm almost at the end of the alleyway when a miaow and clattering behind me make me jolt. I snap around to see a small, dark-coloured cat racing towards me, its eyes gleaming in the reflected light. It stops abruptly, just out of my reach. I crouch and stretch my arm out, clicking my tongue against the roof of my mouth, but the animal does not move.

In the distance, there is an elongated yowl. The cat flattens its ears against its head. Then it dives past me, exits the alley and crosses the road, disappearing behind a wheelie bin. The wailing ceases and another feline emerges from the end of the alley, travelling at speed, until the sight of me stops it in its tracks.

This cat is larger than the first, and even in the artificial light, it's striking; an elegant long-haired breed. It arches its back, fluffing its tail up like a brush, then drops its belly to the ground. It slinks past me, keeping close to the wall. Then, increasing its speed again, it follows the first animal behind the bin. A cacophony of spitting and squalling commences, followed by a series of thuds, as the fighting felines thrash against the plastic receptacle.

I march across the road and utter a low, determined "No!" The racket continues. I lift the lid of the wheelie bin and bang it shut three times, shouting "Pack it in". Both cats fly out from behind it, the smaller one heading to the right, while its assailant races off in the opposite direction, pausing in front of the next street light in the row.

I continue on, assuming that the long-haired cat will make its getaway when I get too close for comfort, but it stands its ground. As I step onto my garden path and close the gate behind me, the animal sneaks up to the metalwork and peers at me through the gaps. I rummage through my handbag for my door keys, nervous about turning my back on the creature, although I'm not sure why.

I pull the keys out of my bag and unlock the door. As I step inside, I glance back. The cat is still there, bathed in the light from the street lamp. It creases its mouth into a snarl as I shut the door.

By the time I've climbed the stairs to the bedroom a few minutes later, I've collected myself enough to be able to smirk at the thought of a cat managing to unsettle me. Nonetheless, before I close the curtains, I scan the street to check it's no longer there.

#

The heat of the sun soaks into the back of my neck and shoulders as I kneel in the grass, removing chickweed from a border with a trowel. At least, I think it's chickweed. My gardening skills are hit and miss at best. I sit back, pick up the water bottle beside me and unscrew the cap. As I sip the lukewarm liquid, an odd sensation overwhelms me; the feeling that I am being watched. I twist around to find a black cat surveying me from the roof of next door's shed.

An image of my journey home from the office summer party two weeks ago flashes through my mind. Is this the same cat that fled from its enemy that night? The neighbourhood is full of cats though, so it's impossible to be sure. I rise and walk towards it, trowel and water bottle in hand.

21

"Was it you that nasty cat was chasing? I hope he didn't hurt you. Did he? No? Good."

The cat doesn't move a muscle and I feel my cheeks burn, conscious that I am talking out loud. I clean the soil off the trowel, before returning it to my own shed, and retreat into my airy kitchen.

I head to the cupboard for a glass, fill it with fresh water, and amble over to the fridge. I remove the ice cube container from the freezer compartment and pop two ice cubes out of it, relishing the satisfying plop as they hit the water. As I swivel to face the sink again, I inhale sharply, my heart skipping a beat at the sight of a face at the window. Then I laugh. It is only the cat.

She — for some reason, I assume it's a she — parades from one end of the windowsill to the other, nuzzling her face against the brickwork at each end. She doesn't have a collar or identity tag, and she's scrawnier than I'd initially thought. Her fur is speckled with mud and I wonder whether she's a stray. Tempted though I am to let her in, I don't want to steal someone else's precious pet, so I leave her to it and exit the room. When I come back later, she has gone.

#

I'm snuggled up on the sofa in front of the television, a cup of tea on the table next to me. It isn't dark outside yet, but I've pulled the curtains across the window and the patio doors, and switched the table lamps on. The electric fan next to the television sweeps from side to side, the gentle whoosh it produces reassuring in its regularity, while the soft breeze it emits is a refreshing relief from the humidity.

The soundtrack of the film on the television fades into the distance as I doze. I'm no longer in the living room, but somewhere dark and dank. Water drips from the ceiling, and my feet are bare and covered in grime. The eerie sound of fighting cats echoes through the night air. Something moves in the shadows…a glint of yellow eyes…I search for a way out and —a

A rattling pulls me from my dream world. Something is trying to get through the small window next to the patio doors. The curtains are moving and a shape is visible behind them. I freeze as I try to adjust to my wakened state and work out what it is. A plaintive miaow and I realise that a cat is clambering in.

I rush over to the window and throw the curtains back. A bundle of black fur flies through the window, leaps from the sill and shoots across the room, taking cover behind the sofa. As I shut the window, a tiny, tortoiseshell cat springs onto the outside ledge and reaches its paws up. There is a hideous screeching noise as it trails its claws down the glass. Unable to keep its balance, it tumbles from the windowsill. I watch it for a moment as it stalks up the path, then I draw the curtains again. I head towards the sofa to try and coax the kitty out from behind it.

Despite my attempts, she refuses to emerge. I consider shoving the sofa forward and forcing her to come out, but decide she's had enough scares for one evening. Instead, I take my cup into the kitchen and make some fresh tea. I'm pouring the steaming water into the cup when I notice the cat in the doorway. I carry on with what I'm doing, trying not to alarm her, and my patience is rewarded.

She sidles in, padding across the tiled floor. She brushes past my legs and back again, purring loudly. I'm loath to feed her, as she isn't mine, and I don't have any pet food anyway. Nor, however, do I want to send her back outside to face the tortoiseshell terror if it's still lurking nearby. The kitchen window doesn't face the garden and the glass of the back door is frosted, so I head back to the living room, the cat just inches behind me. As I approach the patio doors, she halts in the middle of the room.

"Come on, you. You're safe in here."

I peek through the curtains. The light is fading, but not only is the tortoiseshell cat visible on the path, two other felines are sitting on the wall that separates the garden from the back alley. The long-haired hissing fury I'd encountered two weeks ago stands in front of the doors. He's bigger than I remember, even more impressive, and he wears a collar studded with red diamante-style stones.

A scuffling distracts me and I drop the curtains back. The black cat has fled behind the sofa again. I turn my attention to the garden. Did I just imagine the animals outside? I lift the curtain again and the tableau is revealed for a second time. They are really there. I back away from the doors and address the cat in my home.

"Well, I'm not sending you out there tonight."

Something in my tone soothes her and she emerges from her hiding place. She follows me back into the kitchen. I search the fridge and rummage through the cupboards, trying to find something she can eat. Eventually, I discover a can of tuna lurking behind the baked beans. I empty the fish onto a saucer and place it on the floor. While she gulps the tuna down, I fetch a small bowl from another cupboard and fill it with water. I put it next to the food and, when she's cleared the plate, she laps the liquid up. Finally, she strides into the hall and marches up the stairs, as if she has lived here all her life.

I switch everything off downstairs and head into my bedroom to find her curled up on the bed. I feel guilty about disturbing her, but she's filthy and I suspect she's covered in fleas. Once I've used the bathroom, I pick her up and put her in the hall.

"Sorry, Mrs, you're not staying in there. You can sleep out here or downstairs."

I close the door and clamber into bed. For a few minutes, all I hear is pitiful crying and scratching outside, but eventually there is silence. I curl up on my side and close my eyes.

#

I'm woken by a loud bang. For a moment, I wonder whether someone has broken in. I reach for my phone in case I need to call the police, but it's not on the bedside table. I must have left it downstairs. I sit up, listening for movement, but everything is still. I slide out of bed, slip my dressing gown on and open the bedroom door as quietly as possible. I tip-toe along the hallway and sneak down the stairs. As I reach the bottom and turn the corner, I see someone crouching on the kitchen floor. A sound escapes me, something between a squeak and a groan.

I back up against the wall by the front door and consider making a bolt for it. Would I be able to unlock the door and flee before the intruder reached me? I stare at the lock, then back at the kitchen, trying to work it out, but then I realise that the figure on the floor has gone. In its place is the cat.

The door to the living room is closed, and there is no way that an intruder could have opened it and entered without me seeing them. There isn't room for anyone to hide in the kitchen without being visible from the hallway either. Surely they can't have escaped through the back door or window in an instant and without a sound?

I search for something to use as a weapon, but there's nothing nearby. I move down the hallway, reach around the kitchen doorway and feel for the light switch. I press it and the light comes on. There's nobody there. The window is shut and locked. The back door is secure. The kitchen bin is on its side though, with its lid off, and its contents are strewn across the floor.

I check the living room but nothing is amiss. The figure was obviously nothing more than a trick of the light. The cat must have knocked the bin over scavenging for food. As I return to the kitchen, the animal slinks past me into the hallway. I clear up the mess and wash my hands, while the cat watches from the mat by the front door. I shut the kitchen door behind me as I leave the room and scowl at the creature as I march up the stairs.

"That room's out of bounds too. And there's no point looking at me like that, it's your own fault".

I clamber into bed again. The next thing that wakes me is the beeping of the alarm clock.

#

The cat is waiting on the front doorstep when I get home from work. I open the door and she trots in.

"Out." I gesture at the street as I put my keys back in my bag. "Skeddadle."

She sits in the hallway, washing herself. She's so adorable, I can't bring myself to evict her. Anyway, I still don't know if she has anywhere to go. I shut the door and walk past her into the kitchen. Plonking my bags on the worktop, I gaze down at my uninvited house guest.

"We're going to have to take you to the vet to see if you have one of those fancy chips. Then we can work out whether or not you belong to someone."

The cat ignores me and scrubs her face with her paw.

I remove four cans of cat food and a box of biscuits from one of the carrier bags on the worktop. I rattle the packet of biscuits, and she stops cleaning herself and stares at me.

"Got your attention now, have I? Good. Well, fleas are not welcome here and it would be nice if you were a little more presentable, so I'm afraid we're going to have to do something about both of those things if you want to stay here tonight."

I take a bottle of flea shampoo out of the bag and wave it at her. She shoots me a contemptuous look and slinks into the living room.

"You're not getting out of it that easily", I call after her. "It's bath night, Mrs, whether you like it or not."

#

As it turns out, she doesn't like it one bit and makes her feelings clear throughout the process. She forgives me after she's had her fill of premium chicken in jelly with beef-flavoured biscuits though, and is soon curled up on my lap, purring so loudly that I have to turn the volume on the television up.

Now that she's clean, I notice rips and scars on the edges of her ears, which I assume are the results of fights with other cats in the neighbourhood. I wonder why she's involved in so many scraps. Is it because she's a stray? Or is she just a troublemaker, not an innocent victim? She wakes as I pick her up and move her onto the sofa, but curls up on the cushion as I leave the room to go to bed. Perhaps she was listening to my lecture about the house rules last night after all.

#

It's still early when I wake, but my throat is dry, so I venture downstairs. I pour myself a glass of water and take a sip, before heading back out into the hall.

Tap-tap-tap.

The noise is coming from the living room. The door is ajar. I push it tentatively, and switch the main light on.

Tap-tap-tap.

Someone or something is knocking on the patio doors.

I pull the curtain aside. Dawn is breaking and I see the man before me clearly. I hear him perfectly too, despite the thick glass between us.

"Let me in." His voice is calm yet firm.

"No," I say, although for some reason, I can't move away from the door.

"Where is she? I know she's been here."

"I don't know who you mean." Something about him is strange. Stranger than anything I have ever encountered before.

His hair is almost silver, streaked through with black and blonde, but he is only in his mid or late 20s. He wears a curious, strap-like necklace, dotted with what look like rubies, although I'm sure they can't be real. There are more rich red gems on his jacket in place of buttons, as well as on his shirt collar and his pristine leather shoes. His eyes are a peculiar shade of yellow. He must be wearing coloured contact lenses.

"I want to come inside." It's a command rather than a request.

I shake my head.

"Come outside then." He cocks his head and curves his lips into a welcoming smile. "Your friend is with us. Come and play."

They step forward, the rest of them. I'm not sure where they have come from, or why I haven't noticed them until now. A diminutive woman with short hair shaded with blonde, chocolate and cinnamon tones; a slender, older man with ice-white locks and gleaming amber eyes; a striking ginger-haired boy in his late teens.

"My friend?"

"Your sleek black cat. We have her with us. Come and find her."

"You've taken my cat? Why? Is she hurt? Have you done something to her?"

I reach for the bolt that holds the doors in place and slide it back, turn the key in the lock, and push the right-hand door open. As I place one foot on the patio, his features contort and he hisses at me. I am frozen with fear.

I sense movement behind me and fingers grasp my wrist. As I try to jerk my hand back, I hear a woman's voice.

"Come inside and lock the door".

For some reason, I listen to her. I shift my weight onto my back foot and return to the house, and she lets go of my hand. The man in the garden steps towards me but I close the door. He hisses again and makes a curious whining sound. I lock the door and slip the bolt back into place, each movement torturously slow. My limbs feel as if they are coated with wet cement. The man races up the path and leaps over the garden fence, though the others remain where they are. I draw the curtains and focus my attention on the woman in my house.

For a moment, everything is unnaturally still. She is shorter than me and her head is shaven, apart from a long plait of dark locks, which reaches to her waist. She wears a faded black sleeveless t-shirt and black trousers, while her feet are bare. Her eyes trouble me most, however. Emerald green, flecked with black. They remind me of someone. I just can't place…

The answer dawns on me as her transformation begins. She flickers like a hologram, appearing and disappearing for fractions of seconds at a time. One moment, she is a woman, the next a black cat. The two figures merge, in a tangle of limbs and fur, until the woman is gone and the cat remains.

Panic grips hold of me and I charge into the hall. I open the front door, but the long-haired cat with the red diamante collar sits on the doorstep, blocking my way. I contemplate leaping over him, but the air around him starts to shimmer, like a dark heat haze, and he begins to switch from cat to man and back again. A choir of wailing cats serenade me from somewhere in the street. I slam the door and speed up the stairs.

Somehow, the feline woman has got past me. She blocks the bedroom door, in human form again now. Dropping to her knees, she reaches out and makes a strange clacking sound. I watch her, unsure what to do.

"You aren't real". My words are barely audible.

"Real." She rolls the 'r', the vibration carrying through the rest of the word. "Yes. Real."

"I'm dreaming. People don't change into cats."

"People, no. Us, yes."

"Us?"

She sits back, her hands on the tops of her thighs. "My kind".

"Your kind?" I curl my lip, more with annoyance at myself for being unable to do more than repeat her than anything.

"We were from another world." She focuses on every word she utters, as if translating from another tongue. "At first, we lived apart from you. Amid the deserts. Mountains. Trees. Now we are amongst you. We live off things you give us…leave behind."

She yawns, opening her mouth wide. Her throat is coated in something thick and tarry. It reminds me of the bottom of an ashtray that has been left unwashed for months, and I recall the upturned bin and the rubbish that lines the alley by the railway arches.

"What do you want from me?" The wailing outside reaches a crescendo. "The others? Are they the same as you?"

"Yes. No." She snarls the words. "They live in houses. Wear collars. Chase ones like me away."

"Why?"

"Territory. Snobbery. They do not think we belong near them."

"Oh." Anger rises within me. Have I been in danger because of her? She rescued me from them, true, but if she hadn't entered my home, surely they wouldn't have been interested in me at all?

She senses my annoyance. "Not all cats are us. We are not all cats. But those you saw tonight are not safe to be near."

"Well, I didn't have any trouble until you arrived."

She shrugs. "They bring bad luck eventually. Nightmares. Darkness. Not yet, maybe. But soon."

I shiver at the recollection of my dream of the dark place and the otherworldly eyes. "And you don't?"

"No." She stands. "And I will not stay."

"You mean you like living out there? On your own? With nobody to take care of you?"

Her laugh is a deep rumbling purr.

"Yes. Not a pet. Not owned. I like freedom."

I think about the cat food in the kitchen and pang of sadness overcomes me. "Are you sure you don't want to stay? For a little while, at least?"

She shakes her head. "I will go. When the light is brighter. When most of them are in their homes."

"Will they come after me? Keep following me?"

"If you see them, as cats or humans, tell them this. 'Begone, spirit, I will not bow to your will.' Those words have" — she pauses, searching for the right phrase — "power."

I can't think of anything else to say. I am suddenly conscious of how much my muscles hurt, how weary I feel.

Her mouth stretches into a grin.

"Sleep," she says, and steps aside from the bedroom door. I enter the room, remove my dressing gown and crawl under the duvet. As I drift off, I feel the unmistakable weight of a cat jumping onto the bed.

#

When I wake up, I'm alone. Scenes from my dreams flood into my mind. People in the garden, a cat on the front step, a woman shifting into an animal. It all seems ridiculous now, as the sunlight streams in through the gap between the curtains, warming my bare legs, yet it was so vivid.

I get out of bed and reach for my dressing gown. I put it on, tie the belt and then retrieve my slippers from their usual place by the dressing table. I head downstairs into the kitchen, put the kettle on and open the living room door.

It's cooler than I expect and, as I draw the curtains back, I see why. The small window, through which the cat first entered my home, is open. I obviously forgot to close it before I went to bed. There's no sign of her. She must have gone out during the night.

The long-haired, diamante-collared cat sits on the garden wall, a supercilious expression on its face. It closes its eyes dismissively and I remember something from last night. The words the woman said had power. Superstitious nonsense. Just gibberish from a dream. Yet I feel compelled to say them anyway.

"Begone, spirit, I will not bow to your will."

The cat's ears twitch and it swishes its tail. One final glare and it disappears over the wall. I feel something lift from me, as if I am casting off a heavy, invisible cloak. Somehow, I know my beautiful black cat will never return, but I also know the long-haired cat and his companions won't come near my home again. This is my territory now.

Anya J. Davis juggles a job with running a copywriting business and writing horror/fantasy fiction. An Open University graduate, she lives in Devon, in the South West of England.

She has had short stories published in Massacre Magazine and by World Weaver Press, and another was long-listed for the 2016 Exeter Writers Short Story competition. She is currently working on a novel. You can find her on Twitter (@traumahound23) or read more short stories on her blog: www.anyajdavis.wordpress. com

A Sunset Companion
By Mark Cassell

Moments after a car crash, Alfred learns that there is much more to his black cat sighting.

From sunlight to darkness in mere seconds. Squealing tyres, shrieking metal. And silence…

Alfred opened his eyes but only blurred light greeted him, jagged and confusing. The stink of burnt rubber and damp foliage clogged his nostrils. He coughed and an ache raced through his brain. Seconds dragged as his vision sharpened the sunset. The sound of tinkling glass lanced his eardrums, and he tried to move. His seat belt restricted him.

Then he remembered: Martha hadn't worn her seat belt.

Thank the Lord she was still with him, wide-eyed and pretty as always—her senior years had been so very kind. Regardless of not wearing her restraint, she looked fine if a little dazed.

Somewhere above them, birds chirped. Those shrill cries drilled into his head. He winced.

Often he would tell Martha—remind her—to fasten her seat belt, and she would always respond that she never found them comfortable. This went back to the mid-70s when a Road Traffic Bill was put forward in the House of Commons, coinciding with those 'Clunk-Click' TV commercials. He remembered the fuss she made when it became compulsory should the car have them fitted.

"What a silly idea!" she had said at the time. "Strapped in like children."

The right side of his head hurt like hell. He rubbed his face and his hand came away wet and red. The rest of his body felt fine other than a few familiar aches; for the past decade his body woke up to all sorts of discomfort. Yet he could not complain, he was more able-bodied than the majority of his peers and, moreover, his mind remained sharp.

The windscreen was a patchwork of cracks. His door window however was unbroken, beyond which he saw the cat. Again. Not your average domestic cat, but much larger. It now crouched in the darkness of thorny bushes, blending with the shadows. Could it be a panther? Dear God, really? He had heard of black cat sightings in the area, although shrugged them off as ridiculous urban legends. Bloody thing was the reason why he crashed. He had been the one driving, Martha beside him, when the large cat bounded across the road. Black fur glistening, eyes reflecting the sunset like cooling embers; a sudden dark streak across the tarmac. Alfred had swerved.

And here they were, his car a wreck, mangled bonnet around the trunk of a looming oak.

With rubber fingers, he released his seat belt. The metal clasp smacked the central pillar. Shifting sideways, still aware of the cat's presence, he looked at his wife. Being such a law-abiding English gentleman, he had soon gave seat belts little thought and found himself clunking and clicking. They were not in any way uncomfortable as Martha protested. Several years ago he read somewhere that on the 40th anniversary of Clunk-Click over 100,000 lives had been saved. He wondered what the tally was now, himself and Martha included in those numbers.

"It's okay," he whispered and took Martha's hand.

It was relatively easy to clamber from the wreckage, and even when they were both clear he didn't once lose his grip on her. They stood looking at the Toyota's crumpled bonnet and mashed grill. Steam hissed. Wispy phantoms crawled up the bark.

The cat—the panther, whatever it was—was no longer nearby. A quick scan of the surrounding trees and shrubs and tangle of brambles, revealed nothing. Still that warmth filled him. Fear of the cat or anger at crashing, he could not tell.

Martha wasn't saying much, nor could he blame her. It was he who had been driving, he was to blame, taking a shortcut through country lanes at a time of day where the low sun bleached the world pale and bright. Martha had been talking about their plans for when they returned home.

"Don't get me wrong," she was saying, "I've truly enjoyed our weekend, it's just I miss having time away from home. I'd like us to book another break, further away and for longer. Not just one week but perhaps two. We need to make the most of these years, Alfred, while we're still in good health."

He saw her point. If only she could see his when it came to wearing that seat belt. Sometimes he annoyed himself and he doubted that he would ever give up thinking of her safety.

Now he was walking with her, away from the car wreck. And that cat. The sunset blinked through the branches of the autumnal canopy and they eventually came to a stream cut between the immense oaks. Without pause, they stepped into the water. Coldness soaked through to his toes, and he and Martha cleared the stream in two strides. His shoe slipped on the embankment. Martha found it no trouble and remained silent as he composed himself on the other side.

The air damp, the ground swampy, their trek through the woodland became more a zigzag path, avoiding lichen-coated rock and ivy-clad boulders. Some of the boulders were broken, gaping like jagged yawns. Years of forest growth covered each one, and although some were as large as houses, they were dwarfed by the surrounding oak trees.

Over the last few years, Alfred had taken to each day with appreciation. Life was for living. Enjoying. It was sad that there were those out there whom took it upon themselves to end their own lives. What of the driver heading towards the cliff without any intention of braking? Did they, from home to final destination, bother to wear a seat belt? Were they at such an emotional low they clicked the belt into place out of simple habit as opposed to an ironic view of their safety during the oncoming journey? Maybe they wished to avoid any entanglements with the law, and if they considered such things with apparent lucidity then was it not possible to bring themselves out from their most desperate hour?

If only things were as simple as the pleasant stroll he and Martha were now taking.

Parallel with them, the cat broke the shadows between a scattering of smaller rocks. Its eyes again reflecting the sunset—not at all urban legend but real, as sure as his heartbeat. Incredible. Crisp leaves whispered beneath its paws as it kept pace with them.

A small part of him knew he should be afraid, but...

Thinking back to the accident, Alfred squeezed Martha's hand. Still she said nothing, nor did she return his small sign of affection. Was it affection? Guilt, most likely. The sun had been low in the sky and he had reduced his speed accordingly, yet he should have seen the cat sooner. The next moments were lost to darkness...and now he was walking with Martha. Walking away from that darkness.

Just as it had then, the beast leapt across their path. Fur glistened, muscles rippled. It bounded in front and froze between tree trunks on the edge of deepening shadows. A flurry of leaves swirled. That impressive beast huddled in a place where rays of red sunshine failed to penetrate.

The air seemed to shrink in Alfred's throat, and he and Martha jerked to a standstill. He must run, return to the car wreck, he had to call the police, an ambulance... Run, run away...

Those red eyes, not reflecting the sun at all but glowing from an inner fire, locked on his own. A heat surged through his body, similar to that which filled him earlier in the day on the south-east coast; a rare warmth which arrived with a strange October, the two of them appreciating both the weather and the other's company. He was lucky. They were lucky.

From behind them, leaves rustled. Getting louder. Voices too.

Alfred turned.

Two police officers approached between the trees, twigs snapping.

"Sir," one of them shouted. "Stop there!"

Alfred looked back towards the cat. Its eyes burned, blinked once, and it tilted its great head. And then darted off. No more than a dark streak in shadowy folds, it vanished. A chill rushed through him. His fingers and toes numbed and his breath plumed before him in a lazy cloud. He dragged his eyes from the swaying foliage, from what looked like quivering shadow, and peered over his shoulder. His head throbbed.

All he could do was let go of Martha's hand.

One policeman already stood a short distance from Alfred, while the other staggered to a halt further away.

A silence deepened the gloom.

The officer closest to Alfred opened his mouth to say something but his colleague's strangled words stopped him. Alfred frowned and wondered what they both stared at. He followed their gazes, looking down at his feet.

Blood peppered his shoe and soaked into the earth. Next to that was Martha's hand.

"Martha," he said, "you should've worn your seat belt."

Mark Cassell lives in a rural part of the UK with his wife and a number of animals. He often dreams of dystopian futures, peculiar creatures, and flitting shadows. Primarily a horror writer, his steampunk, dark fantasy, and SF stories have featured in numerous anthologies and ezines. His 2015 release, Sinister Stitches, is a collection of stories from a mythos that began with his best-selling debut novel, The Shadow Fabric, a supernatural horror tale of demons, devices, and deceit.

For more about Mark and his work, or to contact him directly:

Free stories: www.markcassell.com
The Shadow Fabric mythos: www.theshadowfabric.co.uk/
Twitter: https://twitter.com/Mark_Cassell
Facebook: www.facebook.com/AuthorMarkCassell
Blog: www.beneath.co.uk/

Little Black Protector
By Steven Van Patten

A man saves a cat, only to find that he's the one that needs rescuing.

"William, have you seen the news?" his mother asked him through the cell phone.

"Good morning to you too, mom," he said as he struggled to open his eyes.

"Yes, good morning son," she quipped. She was exasperated by her son's sudden need for her to be cordial and he saw it for the sarcasm that is was. "The thing on the news about the cats, did you see it?"

"See what, mom?"

"The thing on the news about pet cats going crazy!" she shouted. "People are being attacked, and some reports said they're exhibiting higher intelligence. I tell you, this world is just gone crazy... I mean between the Republicans..."

As his mother changed subjects, his eyes came to focus. In his bedroom, lit only in slivers where the blinds covering his windows allowed, the world seemed normal. It wouldn't be until he left the bedroom that all his mother's warnings about Republicans, his forgetting to take his vitamins and killer cats would become relevant.

One thing was for sure; this was probably not a good time to tell his mother than he has had a cat for the past four weeks.

"… and did you start taking those vitamins I gave you?" she asked now that she was done roasting Republicans.

"Yes, mother," he lied. "Hey, I gotta get ready for work. Can we pick this up later?"

"Of course," she said. The subject of work was always a reliable conversation kill switch for whenever he'd had enough of being cautioned of the world's perils. From his mother's tone one would think he were some big breasted blonde about to go inside a haunted house, instead of a 5'10" semi-muscular black man headed to work to process invoices.

They said their goodbyes as he sat up and looked around. His bedroom door was still closed; leaving him to wonder if the black tabby he'd left in his living room was waiting on the other side, filled with malicious intent.

"Figures," he muttered to himself as he reflected on how he ended up with a cat in the first place. All he did was tell a co-worker that he'd been thinking about getting a pet, what with the recent break-up he'd experienced leaving his apartment feeling a little empty. The next day the well-meaning co-worker shows up at his cubicle with an animal carrier and a sad story about a woman who had fallen ill and could no longer care for an 8-year old black cat named Carla. The only other choice would have been to take Carla to a shelter. "And you know after a couple of weeks, they'd put Carla to sleep!"

"How'd you even get an animal past building security?" William had asked.

"That's not the point," Bridgette insisted. "I would take her, except I already have two cats and they would end up killing Carla. They actually tried to last night. I had to keep her locked in my bathroom all last night. Come on! Just look at her!"

And he did. He peered through the carrier's plastic mesh and saw the sweet little cat face. Carla was as black as an ace of spades, which to him was a selling point. And it wasn't just that the cat was cute, it was the sadness welled up in those supernatural green eyes. The very sight of her face literally broke his heart. He'd never in his life been that closely confronted by an animal in need before, and it woke a sudden heroism in him. Of course, he knew he was being suckered, but he supposed there was nothing wrong with being suckered to save a defenseless animal. At least, that was his thought at that moment.

At the end of his workday, there he was walking past the security desk with the carrier. "Hey! You know you're not supposed to have that thing in here!"

"Yeah, I know," he said without breaking stride or even looking at the guard who had somehow managed to miss the carrier when Bridgette brought it into the building.

Before he left the office, Bridgette, (who knew him a little better than either of them would be comfortable to admit) would add, "You don't have to worry about her. She's a very independent, aloof cat. She'll find a space to be comfortable on one side of your apartment and will leave you to your business."

In the weeks to come, that promise would turn out to be the biggest lie a woman he wasn't sleeping with had ever told him.

As he rode the Brooklyn-bound 3 train that would eventually get him home, Carla had become frightened and began howling terribly. He tried to reassure her gently, more concerned about people complaining about the noise than anything else.

All I need is some old, Trump-supporting white lady calling PETA on me! 'There's this horrible black man mistreating a cat! He should be beaten publicly and deported! What? I don't care if he's an American citizen!'

Fortunately for him, the natural paranoia that sometimes comes with being a person of color living in New York City went unrealized, as he was neither confronted nor accosted during his commute. The feline's protests did earn him a few stares on the way home. Most of the stares dripped of disapproval, but the sight of a man willing to care for a pet actually moved one female passenger. She didn't have the nerve to approach him during the train ride, but would post an ad in the 'Missed Connections' section of Craig's List later that night. In the ad, she'd playfully refer to him as 'the handsome black man with the angry pussy ' and offer to buy him a cup of coffee. Unfortunately, he wasn't a Craig's List person and missed the post entirely.

Once in the apartment and freed from the carrier, the cat ran for the couch and hid under it for some time. He eventually managed to coax her out with deli-style turkey slices and the cat seemed to calm down. Then began the exploration, as the cat strolled across the furniture getting acclimated with her surroundings. Meanwhile, he trailed behind her, snatching up glue traps, sharp objects and fragile valuables that were in the path of his new houseguest.

A quick trip to Duane Reade satisfied the need for kitty litter, a litter box and more importantly, cat food. For the first night, the cat seemed content with lounging in the living room while he rested in his bedroom. Everything seemed to be going very well.

It wasn't until the next evening that he realized that there was a potential problem. He'd just spent his customary ten hours in the office and another two scoffing down Heinekens while a large-breasted waitress pretended to flirt with him. Carla greeted him as he entered his front door. There she was, sitting on her hind legs, looking even sadder than when he peered at her in the carrier.

And that's where the 'meowing' began, over and over until he'd gotten himself settled and petted the creature for a few minutes. As he looked down on her, he could see the sadness melt away as something else seemed to fill the black-furred face. Was it adoration or just humility in the face of a new 'parent'? Hard to say, but in those few minutes a corner had definitely been turned.

As the days progressed, Carla the Cat would continue to appear annoyed at him anytime he was absent from the apartment for longer than three hours. And while he was home, she would be anything but aloof. Carla followed him around as if she was his secret service detail: 'We're in the living room! No wait, now we're in the kitchen. Wait! Stand by! The Package is now in the bedroom!'

Sometime after that, the sneezing started. As it turned out, he was mildly allergic to cats. The strength of his condition was nothing life threatening, but definitely an inconvenience considering the cat's demeanor. That's when he banned her from the bedroom, figuring he would endeavor to keep the rest of the apartment clean, but would need one fur-free zone in order to sleep in peace.

Carla didn't seem to mind being forbidden from the bedroom as much as she seemed to resent restrictions in general. In the days that followed, she would greet him at the bedroom door first thing in the morning, expressing her discontent with either meows or growls. He'd come to suspect that the meows were the mix of a basic greeting and inquiry regarding turkey slices, while the growls were testament of Carla's annoyance over his not being available for petting during the course of the night.

He rose out of bed, went to the bedroom door, and pressed his ear to it. Silence. So there he stood, his heartbeat quickening as he decided whether or not to heed his mother's warning.

His hand wrapped around the doorknob, as he readied himself to close it immediately if the cat were to suddenly leap at him. If she's gone crazy, I'll just hit her with the door, he thought.

He opened the door slowly, just a few inches so he could peer out with his left eye. There was nothing but the empty hallway that led to rest of the apartment.

Disgusted at himself for letting his mother's latest Amber Alert get the better of him, he swung the door open and headed to the bathroom. As he relieved himself, he listened intently to hear if the cat was heading his way. Now, he reasoned, would be the perfect time to attack. Thankfully, the apartment remained still as he could only imagine the indignity of being found on the toilet, murdered by household pet.

It wasn't until he'd finished his shower and pulled the plastic curtain back that he saw the cat, sitting on her butt in the bathroom doorway. She meowed at him.

This sort of thing had happened before, so it was not out of the ordinary. However, with no door between them and his imagination running like Carl Lewis in the '80s, now he had to think of what he'd do if the cat should attack while all he had available to defend himself were towels and a damp ass.

"Hi, Carla!" he said with forced cheer. The cat made no reaction, but continued to study him.

He took a deep breath and sighed. Shit, this cat better not mess with me, he thought as he took the first step out of the shower.

Carla stood up, turned as if suddenly disinterested and scampered away, presumably to the living room.

He fantasized about visiting his mother's condo and destroying her cable TV box, thereby slaying the source of all the fears she'd heap upon him as he dried off hastily and stomped back to his bedroom to get dressed.

Fifteen minutes later, he had finished replenishing the cat's food and water and began scrambling eggs with white cheddar cheese, pepper and paprika for himself. The cat joined him in the kitchen and sniffed the dry cat food in her bowl, then watched him pull strips of turkey bacon out of the microwave and combine them on his plate with the eggs. He stood by the stove and they ate, each of them stealing glances at one another the whole time. Minus the way the eggs were prepared, this had been the second half of their morning routine for a month.

Finally letting go of the notion that his mother's warnings had any validity, he finished his food, turned to the sink and washed the plate. Afterwards, there was nothing left to do but grab his knapsack and head towards the door.

"See ya, Carla!" he shouted casually.

He was about four feet away from his front door when the cat suddenly bolted past him, and turned as if to block his path. With her back hunched up in what is typically regarded as a hostile stance in felines, Carla bared her impressive set of incisors and hissed.

Oh my God! This cat is going to make me kill her!

Alarmed, he remembered that his mother said the cats who had attacked their owners had become super intelligent. It was at this moment he wanted to kick himself in the ass for not turning on the news when his mother first called. If he survived this, he realized that he might actually owe his mother an apology.

"Well, if you've really gone all super-intelligent, Dawn of The Planet of The Apes on me, then maybe I'll just get something off my chest, you clingy little pain in my ass!" He scoffed as he lowered himself down on one knee and locked eyes with Carla:

"Here is the thing! I'm glad you like me and I like you. But the reality of the situation is that I can't take care of you if I don't go to work. Humans feed themselves, their families and their pets by making money. Now, without money I can't feed you, can't keep a roof over our heads and protect you. So you're going to have to get used to me being gone sometimes. This is how the world works. Now get out of the way!"

By the time he'd gotten halfway through his diatribe, his words had lost some of their conviction, as he slowly came to realize that the cat wasn't hissing at him anymore. In truth, was she was 'shushing' him. "I am not stopping you because I'm lonely, you stupid man! I'm stopping you because there's a demon outside."

"Oh fuck!" he exclaimed as his life suddenly stopped making sense. *I must be dead. That's it! I'm dead or I'm dreaming!*

The most disturbing part was that Carla's voice didn't sound like anything the movies or television had conditioned him to expect from a talking cat. There was no sexy drawl, no rolling of the 'r's, no motherly Madge Sinclair from The Lion King. If anything, Carla sounded like an old school action hero who smoked too many cigarettes back when Reagan was president.

"I have a job," Carla continued. "I protect humans from demons."

"Demons?" he parroted.

"Yes, William! Demons!" Carla seemed irritated at having to repeat herself for the sake of what was supposed to be a creature with intellect superior to hers. "Citizens of Hell, if you will."

"How? Why? And why here?" he asked.

"I don't know, but she's in the hallway. She'll probably pretend to be a religious person."

As if on cue, a knock on the door startled William so badly that he jumped backwards.

"Hello?" a voice called from behind the door. "I'd like to share some good news with you!"

Jehovah's Witness! I've got a demon outside my door pretending to be a Jehovah's Witness!?

He shook himself as if trying to wake from a nightmare, but nothing changed. This brought him to another conclusion.

I'm hallucinating! Somebody must have slipped me something... but I didn't go out last night... did I? Maybe it's the allergy medicine! Yeah, it's that fucking Allegra!

"Open the door," he heard Carla whisper.

"Why would I do that?" Oh man! Now I AM the dumb chick in the horror movie! Or the cat is!

The knocking continued, quickly evolving into pounding. Wouldn't a real Jehovah's Witness have gone away by now?

"I NEED TO TALK TO YOU ABOUT YOUR SOUL!!!" the voice called, as it seemed to warble and deepen.

Dust and small paint chips flew off the door's edges from the blows.

"Open the door!"

He stepped left as Carla pounced right. "Really?" he asked as his trembling hands reach for the locks.

"DO IT!"

The top lock clicked open. The bottom lock clicked open. He felt light-headed, as if he were in the early stages of an outer-body experience. The doorknob burned under his touch.

The door flew open, suddenly pushed hard by 'The Witness'. Except for the glowing red eyes and the smell of sulfur, she looked like any of the other middle-aged West Indian ladies he'd ever walked past as he ran errands in his south Brooklyn neighborhood.

The demon seemed to lunge, but stopped short at the sight of Carla. The glow from the monster's red eyes intensified and widened with what appeared to be anger married to fright.

It took a second for William to realize that the black thing that whizzed by his head was in fact, Carla. The attack was fast and sudden and no sooner had the cat launched into the air than was she running in the opposite direction past his feet.

Not realizing that the demon was already well on her way to dying, William almost turned to yell at Carla for not finished the creature off. But a scratch was apparently all it took. Four tiny slices in the demon's left cheek opened and spread across its face like some sort of flesh-eating bacteria. The creature's skin pulled apart, dissolved and melted. Muscles liquefied and bones burst into powder as the screaming hellion fell to its knees. In the end, there was nothing left but a pungent puddle of black tar.

After a moment, he let the door close and turned back to Carla. They stared at each other for a minute before she finally spoke.

"If there aren't any more demons in the immediate area, I will eventually revert back to my old self. I'll definitely be back to normal by the time you get home from work. I won't be able to talk again until the next crisis, so don't expect it. But I did want to say thank you for the food and the comfort. You're a great father."

"You're welcome!" William responded. It felt good to have his efforts acknowledged.

The cat turned to go back in the living room, then seemed to remember something. "One last thing before you go to work. I'm horny as hell! Could you get me a boyfriend?"

Oh shit! This cat isn't fixed?!

"Kidding! Just wanted to see the look on your face!" Carla said. She seemed to flash him a mischievous smile before she turned and leaped out of view.

Although he couldn't see himself, he could only imagine how dumbstruck he must have looked. It seemed like a long time before he finally opened the front door again and stepped to the other side, but it had only been a minute. He was careful to avoid the puddle of goo as he exited. The super is not going to like this, he thought.

A half hour later he was still so shell-shocked that he missed his stop on the subway, ending up in Times Square instead of Penn Station. That mishap would make him a half-hour late for work and force him to tell a very creative, yet more palatable, lie to his boss.

Steven Van Patten is the author of the Brookwater's Curse vampire novel series and Killer Genius: She Kills Because She Cares, which was nominated by the African American Literary Award Show in the category of Best Mystery/Suspense Novel for 2016. He lives in Crown Heights Brooklyn, with his cat, Lola. Steven also stage manages television shows when he's not writing. Find out more about Steven at The Laughing Black Vampire. http://www.brookwaterscurse.com/

Roof Cats
By Jonathan Broughton

Shocking things can happen when you try to be a good neighbor.

Terry Nugent spun the washing machine dial to D. Short wash and long spin, forty-five minutes. More than enough time to phone the RSPCA and complain about his next door neighbour.

Where he lived on Magdalen Road, five storey Victorian houses made up a short terrace. The utility window in his fifth floor flat looked out across their roofs. Ten days ago, next door, two cats appeared. One, black and white, the other a tortoiseshell.

Surprised, then worried, then shocked, he wondered that anyone with an ounce of sense thought to keep cats in a top floor flat.

On their first day, the cats emerged from his neighbour's open window and gazed at their new airy surroundings. Then, tentative at first, they stepped out onto the sloping roof and inched their way towards the gutter and a seventy-foot drop to the ground. He wanted to call, to shoo them off, but scared they'd take fright and bolt... and slip... he stared, rooted to the spot and, in his head, wished them away.

After what seemed an age, they slunk back to the window and, bolder now, climbed the roof that belonged to the neighbour's neighbour. At the top, a flat ledge divided the roof in two and there the cats sat and blinked, unafraid of the yawning abyss on either side.

Each time a pigeon flew past, the cats tensed and twice they crouched ready to pounce. 'Remember the stories,' he thought, 'in The Daily Mail, of cats that survive falls from tower blocks.' It didn't help.

That first time, he watched them for three hours. When, at last, they went back through the window, he staggered to his sofa and lay there for so long that dusk fell before he managed to recover. Even then, only a thin minestrone soup with a dry cracker made up his meagre dinner. Nothing more.

Every day, bold and curious, the cats explored their rooftop domain and Terry watched and worried.

His kitchen, built out from the back of the house and with a large flat sloping roof, encouraged the pigeons. The males strutted and cooed and the females feigned indifference or flew away.

And on the opposite roof, the cats crouched, stalked down to the gutter and glared. A tail twitched, whiskers quivered.

Terry's heart pounded. The pigeons swooped past and wheeled left and right, always just out of range of a strike.

'Suppose a pigeon misjudges the distance? The cats won't remember where they are... and then...' It didn't bear thinking about.

Yet he did think about it, all day and every day, and dream about it at night. Every morning, before he filled the kettle for his first cup of coffee, he checked on the cats. The neighbor's window stayed open, day and night (he often peered out during the early hours, unable to sleep) and the cats came and went as they pleased.

Tiredness and worry gnawed at his head and heart. At work, his concentration faltered and his Line Manager picked up on the less than satisfactory written reports that the company's high standards demanded from him at all times.

Terry took two days' sick leave. 'I shall go next door tomorrow,' he decided, 'and make the cats' owner aware of their foolish and slapdash attitude. I shall extract a promise that the cats' welfare be given greater consideration. If this promise isn't forthcoming, I shall have no alternative but to report them to the authorities. I shall spend my second day off in bed, to recover.'

That night, the weather changed. For many days, hot sun bathed the Sussex Downs in warmth, but now it hid behind thick grey clouds that rolled up the English Channel.

From his bedroom window, Terry watched the wind whip the distant waves into white crests. And rain threatened. The clouds rushed along as the gale strengthened. He went back to bed and dozed. 'In nasty weather, cats stay indoors.' And, whoever lived next door would need to shut the window because of the wind. He turned over and dozed off.

An hour later, he crawled out of bed to go and make a cup of coffee, and, as he passed through the utility room, gave a quick glance outside.

The cats clung to the tiles, bodies low, their ears flat, the wind snatching at their fur. He staggered in disbelief.

The neighbour's window stood open, as usual, shuddering in the gale's blast. A net curtain flapped up and over the frame, its bottom edge a muddy grey from where it soaked up splattered seagull dirt.

Terry didn't wash. He flung on yesterday's clothes, thrust the door keys into his jeans pocket and took the stairs two at a time.

Outside, in the playing field on the other side of the road, the chestnut trees' branches thrashed in the frantic wind and torn leaves and broken twigs swirled in circular eddies on the pavement.

'How dare that mad person be so... stupid!' Fury fuelled his resolve and he strode up to his neighbour's front door.

A cluster of door bells with faded and badly written numbers made it difficult to know which one to press. He bunched his hands into fists to keep his head clear.

'My flat is number five.' His flat occupied the top floor. On the bottom button scrawled a faded '5' in black felt-tip ink. No six, or seven, so this five, like his, must be the top flat, so he pressed it.

Ready to answer, he placed his mouth close to the speaker. And waited. Didn't they hear? Didn't the bell work? "Hello." The gale made hearing anything difficult. He pressed the button again and angled his ear up to the speaker. No reply, no static, no... perhaps they were out.

Ten thirty a.m. They might be shopping. They might be at work. Did they work? No, for this house, like another further up the road, housed people on benefits. If they received benefits, then they didn't work and so he pressed the bell for a third time.

He peered through the letter box. Too dark to see much, a threadbare rug, a flight of wooden stairs and a pile of junk mail to the right of the door.

Frustrated and in despair, he rushed back to his house and took the stairs three at a time.

The cats huddled close together beside the open window. Why didn't they jump through? Terry's chest tightened. Blood smears coated their mouths and chests and dotted their whiskers.

He shook. 'The owner's a monster. They beat the cats. That's why they're always on the roof. This has gone on for far too long. I should have realised earlier. The poor things are scared out of their wits.'

Terry took a deep breath. How dare the owner force them out in this weather! Another, deeper breath.

'Complete a simple household task to restore calm.' He might be dismissed as a crank if, when he rang the RSPCA, he came across as frantic and agitated.

He collected his small pile of washing and set the washing cycle to D. 'Ten minutes reporting my neighbour to the RSPCA. Thirty-five to have a coffee, maybe two.' Thirty-five minutes gave him enough time to soothe his nerves and prepare. For when he explained the appalling treatment handed out to these poor creatures, the RSPCA must come. They'd need to force entry if, when they arrived, the owner didn't answer. 'They must be used to that. A big organisation like them. Used to dreadful people who delighted in animal cruelty. Such awful times we live in.'

As he watched, the tortoiseshell stood and, with a quick jump, disappeared through the window.

Terry held his breath, for he expected it to reappear, terrified by the onslaught of savagery that awaited it inside. When, after a minute, it didn't, he expected the black and white cat to follow, but it hunkered down and squinted into the wind.

Of course! The owner waited for the second cat. Inflicting torture on both of them at the same time heightened the enjoyment of their twisted sadism.

'This cat has learnt that outside is safer.' How much abuse had these innocent animals taken? No time to lose.

Terry snatched up his mobile and dialled the number marked in Yellow Pages.

"Good morning, RSPCA. How may I help you?" A girl's voice, pleasant, friendly.

"I want to report the mistreatment of two cats."

"I see." The shuffle of papers and the click of a pen: "May I ask how these cats are being mistreated?"

"I live in a top floor flat," Terry explained. "These cats live next door, if you see what I mean?"

"So, they live in a top floor flat too?"

"That's right. And the owner lets them out on the roof. In fact, they don't go inside because they're too scared, even on a day like this, with a gale. The window's open but they're terrified, because they're beaten by their owner. One has gone in, but not the other. He... or she has learnt to stay outside where it's safer." He took a deep breath. His hands shook. "I'm terrified the wind's going to blow them off."

"You say that one cat has gone inside, but the other hasn't?"

Terry gulped. "The owner's waiting for the black and white one to jump through. They're tortured together and then thrown out again. It's a seventy-foot drop to the ground. I worry that one of them might slip and if they've been injured by the abuse..."

The girl's voice stayed calm. "Have you seen the owner deliberately mistreat the cats?"

"No — but just now I went round to tell them to get the cats off the roof and they didn't even answer the bell. I mean, normal people shut their windows on windy days. I do. You'd keep a cat in, wouldn't you?"

"Can I ask you, Mr...?"

"Nugent, the name's Nugent, Terry, er... Terrence."

"Mr Nugent — if the cats show any signs of neglect? Do they look underfed? Are they losing their fur?"

Terry peered at the black and white cat. "No — not really." It looked well fed, very well fed. A clear indicator of yet more abuse. "It has plenty of weight, which can't be wise. You can't expect a fat cat to keep its balance on a roof on a windy day. They're being tortured. Please come and remove them for their own safety."

The girl's voice brightened. "That isn't possible, Mr Nugent. We need definite sightings of cruelty before we can apply to have any animal removed."

"What? I told you, their out on the roof, day and night, in all weathers. One slip and they're dead. They daren't go in. They're traumatised."

The shuffle of more papers being re-arranged. "What I will do, Mr Nugent, is keep a record of your call and all your details in our file and ring you back in a few weeks' time to check on the cats' situation. Will that be all right?"

"You mean you're not going to do anything?"

"As I said, we need firm evidence of abuse before we can intervene. In this case, cats walking on a roof in windy weather isn't sufficient." The click of the pen. "May I have your address and telephone number, please?"

When he finished, Terry put down the phone and stared at the cat. 'I tried, I promise. I did my best. Oh no! I didn't tell them about the blood...' Exhausted, failure left his willpower in shreds and he spent the rest of the day in bed.

Next day, the wind dropped. The cats prowled, cleaned their whiskers and basked in the sun. The net curtain, snagged on the window's upper frame, hung limp as a dirty grey rag.

After his good nights' sleep, Terry's spirits revived. The cats, thank goodness, survived the wind. 'Right, I shall ring the police to report the RSPCA's disgraceful attitude.' But — the police, did he really want them involved? Like so many public bodies featured on the TV news, like the RSPCA too, they didn't respond in a pro-active manner, just re-active. Why would they care about the RSPCA's treatment of worried members of the public? They probably didn't care much about cats, either.

Apathy ruled the world. In his little attempt at compassion, he too had failed. So be it. 'A martyr faced by hostile odds maintains their dignity.'

The dish washer, filled with his weeks' dirty crockery, sloshed through the rinse cycle. 'I promise to watch out for the cats. And I shall ring the RSPCA at the first signs of malnourishment or... or whatever. And I shall take that opportunity to rebuke the organisation in the strongest possible terms for not taking action sooner.'

He made a note in his diary of the date and time of yesterday's call and ringed it in red, twice, to remind him to be very angry when he called them again.

Next day, he returned to work. At five p.m. he reported to his Line Manager who congratulated him on his analysis of projected monetary shortfall expected in the next three years if Government funding failed to match expected inflation in the public sector.

Before he left that evening, he went to the canteen for a last coffee. The television showed the local news. No sound, but the running caption read; Police discover woman's remains in top floor flat. Police called to house in Magdalen Road, St Leonards-on-Sea, after residents complain of terrible smell.

As he walked up Magdalen Road, Terry saw the police cars. Saw the white-clad forensic officers enter and leave the house. Had his neighbour been murdered? Saw two large cages on the pavement.

The cats glared at him from behind the cages' wire mesh. The tortoiseshell bared its teeth, flattened its ears and hissed. 'Poor frightened things. Safe now, at last.'

The policeman beside the baskets scowled. "Nasty little brutes." He lifted his hand. Traces of blood soaked through a bandage wrapped tight around his wrist. "Tried to take my hand off."

"What will happen to them?"

The policeman sniffed. "Who knows."

Back in his flat, Terry stood by the utility room window. Pigeons occupied the flat ledge where the cats once sat. The dirty net curtain had been unhooked, the window closed. He ate his sardines on toast without enjoyment.

The following week, the local paper, The Observer, ran his neighbour's death as its headline story:

Horror in Tragic Accidental Death.

The Coroner's autopsy on the body of a woman found in a top floor flat in Magdalen Road, St Leonards-on-Sea, recorded a verdict of accidental death. On an unspecified date, Ms Morris, 48, who suffered from Type 2 diabetes, fell asleep on her bed. She left the bedroom window open for her cats to climb out onto the roof. One, or both of them, came in and, to keep warm, curled up on Ms Morris's face. Death by suffocation ensued. The cats, used to regular meals, ate the deceased.

From that day on, whenever he saw a cat, Terry Nugent crossed the road. If one came too close, he stamped his foot and clapped his hands. If it sat and stared and didn't budge, Terry ran.

Jonathan Broughton: Roof Cats is my one and only cat story and it is based on truth. I live in the top floor flat of a large Victorian house by the sea. My neighbour, in their top floor flat, keeps two cats which she lets out onto the roof. They are quite unfazed by the huge drop to the ground and delight in tormenting the seagulls and pigeons. I don't worry that the cats might fall - not now.

Dark Reunion: Twenty Short Stories includes many of my short stories. There are tales of the paranormal, of horror, a little humour and some that are poignant.

Running Before the Midnight Bell is an urban thriller set in Hastings and St Leonards on Sea, UK. Detective Inspector Anthony Nemo hunts for a killer, a killer who threatens, by the end, to expose his own vulnerabilities.

I wrote *The Russian White* when I still lived in London. Based on the visit of the Russian Tsar, Peter the Great, when he visited Britain at the end of the 17th century and gave, as a gift to King William the Third, a huge uncut diamond. This diamond was lost and I invented a tale, set in Victorian London at the outbreak of the Crimean War, as to why it was lost and the efforts of Russian spies to find it and bring it back to Russia.

In the Grip of Old Winter is a fantasy. It's Christmas. Eleven-year old Peter spends the holidays at his grandparents' strange and ancient house in the middle of a forest. Heavy snow, the heaviest for years, falls and keeps on falling.

Time slips from the present to the deep past. Such cold awakens memories from long-forgotten Ages, ten sixty-six after the Battle of Hastings and further back, to the time of Albion, when mists hid the land and fire-worshippers practiced their arts.

Peter, insecure and fearful, but curious, is thrust into events where the opportunity to change history beckons. There is magic, though it is fickle. There are allies, though he learns fast who he can trust. There is danger, where lives change in dramatic and un-looked for ways. Which, by the end, includes his too.

And through the Ages, the snow falls.

My Amazon Author Page: amazon.com/author/ jonathanbroughton

On Twitter: @jb121jonathan

On Facebook: facebook.com/jonathan. broughton.5

Hell's Kitties
By Phillip T. Stephens

Lucifer needs to quash a goody-two-shoes wreaking havoc in hell. Fortunately, he devised a fool-proof plan. Unfortunately, he designed hell to undermine good fortune....

Lucifer Morningstar lifted his handcrafted Paparazzi XXX trap gun with laser guided sights, GPS tracking and magnetic resonance imaging. Hell's southeastern sun battered his shoulders like twin-barrel blast furnaces. He stood at Station 8 and prepared for his shot.

A squad of eight elite storm troopers stood at attention—perfectly still and forbidden to blink. Normally they wore nothing but weapons, sandals and g-strings. Considering today's heat, however, Lucifer permitted them to appear in full dress uniform.

He trailed Mephistopheles 22 hits to 24. The last time she dared to beat him, over a hand of poker, he sentenced her to thirty millennia in The Hell of Bat Shit Crazy Ex-Spouses Who Never Stop Calling You, or Your Mother, Your New Lover, Your Bosses and Friends to Whine About How Much Better Off You Were With Them.[1] Clearly, she failed to learn her lesson.

---

1 As readers of the novel Raising Hell will know. Lucifer loved to create highly specialized

Hells, sometimes for one person only, with long complicated names and no rational other than

"Pull."

NRA CEO Wayne LaPierre flew from the trap. Lucifer tracked him across the sky and blew him to smithereens. 23-24. He lowered his shotgun and glared at Mephistopheles to remind her Who Ruled Hell and who served at His mercy.

Mephistopheles, his gender bending sibling, leaned on her diamond studded stick seat, which she carried everywhere like a cane. Her left hand balanced a Hellsberg Silver Reserve sporting rifle; the right a triple dry ice and sulfur-dioxide martini with a twist of habeñero pepper. She glanced at her watch with the expression of a housewife during her husband's orgasm—an expression that said, get it over with, I need to finish my cigarette and soap opera before the laundry wrinkles in the dryer.

Lucifer raised his rifle to shoot. "Pull."

Senator Larry Craig sailed from the trap. "Spare me. Send me back. I'll vote to repeal the second amendment." Lucifer's blast shattered him into a thousand pieces. 24-24.

He blew the smoke from the barrel. "Official N.R.A. targets are much more fun than the boring old clay birds."

Lucifer built his range on the backs of minor Vatican clerics who doled out dispensations to poor peasants in the middle ages (peasants who received nothing in return and ended up in hell anyway). He lashed them

---

it pleased him. The arch demon Beelzebub suggested he watched the movie Big Trouble in Little China one too many times, but then Lucifer banished him to the Hell of Watching Bad American Rip-Offs of Second-Rate Hong Kong Kung Fu Movies While Being Subjected to Chinese Water Torture and Listening to Fortune Cookie Fortunes Read Endlessly by Ex-Girlfriends Who Believed They'd Come True.

together and floated them face down in the middle of his favorite lake of lava, which comprised the bowels of the Tamu Massif volcano.

Mephistopheles flipped the gun over her shoulder and stepped to the station for the tiebreaker. She didn't even bother to put down her martini. Her toreador pants and nine-inch spiked heels perfectly matched her camouflaged duck oven jacket.

Lucifer rubbed his scaly palms together. If she missed this shot, he'd win with his.

The trap spat lobbyist Chris Cox like an ICBM. Mephistopheles took a sip of her martini, ran her fingers through her close-cropped fiery red hair and shot the Hellsberg single-handed. The shot clipped Cox, but only slightly. He flew past the beach and over the lava where he disappeared into a sputtering flame.

Lucifer reached under his Monte Cristo Alligator Lizard shooting jacket and scratched his balls with the butt of his Paperazzi. "Miss."

Mephistopheles stomped her right heel into a scholastic's kidney. "I clearly clipped him. He counts."

"He's a lost bird now. Since I'm the official referee, no score."

Mephistopheles cracked the stem of her glass. Since he was Hell's Supreme Lord, she needn't bother to challenge him.

Lucifer stepped back into the station. He opened his mouth. A "p" escaped his lips and the trap released Charlton Heston.

Mephistopheles said, "How's your Pilgrim problem?" Nothing could ruin his shot more than the words "Pilgrim problem."

Only His Almighty Lord It Over You perplexed him more than his Pilgrim problem. Lucifer invested eons into suppressing the pernicious pleasantness of that perpetual do-gooder, yet he always resurfaced to spread help, happiness and harmony.

Heston spiraled past his sights and tumbled across the backsides of a dozen Bishops, priests and papal assistants.

"Tie game, big brother." Mephistopheles opened her cane and poured another drink from the shaft.

Lucifer broke open his shotgun and dropped a shell into his palm from his sleeve. "Misfire. Dud shell."

Mephistopheles, who knew better than to argue, leaned against her cane seat with arms and ankles crossed.

His storm troopers corralled Heston and loaded him back into the trap release.

"As to Pilgrim," he said, "I've pounded that perpetually Pollyannaish pipsqueak into pixie Play-Doh once and for all." He intertwined his fourteen fingers and stretched his palms outward until his knuckles popped like a backfiring car. He retook his position at the station and opened his mouth to call.

Mephistopheles plucked the back hair from a monsignor to stir her drink. "Once and for all? Like the time you asked him to toxify hell's food service and he created GDI Monday's, the most popular franchise ever?"[2] The hair dissolved in the cocktail, leaving only the briefest wisp of smoke.

"Or the time you sent him to New England to incite a War on Christmas and he saved a church from financial

---

2 One of Pilgrim's many exploits readers can enjoy for the bargain basement price of $1 in Raising Hell, also available in paperback.

ruin?"[3] She downed her drink in one gulp. "Or the theme park with booby trapped rides you made him build where he brought joy and happiness to countless children?"[4]

Lucifer recognized her strategy, a stalling tactic American football players called "icing the kicker."

"I sent him to the Hell of the Your Worst Imagination, Where Everything You Feared, Hallucinated, Frightened Gullible Children With or Dreamed Up With Your Stoner Friends Comes to Pass But With Conflicting Rules, Arbitrary Expectations and Unreasonable Demands."

Known in popular proverbs as "The Hell of Your Own Making," Lucifer particularly relished Pilgrim's current sentence. "He'll spend eternity conjuring up his deepest fears in the form of the vilest chimera and monsters from the id. I haven't heard a peep from Pilgrim or his caretaker Bast since I engineered Brexit and Amexodus."[5]

Mephistopheles rolled her eyes so far back into her head she had to cough them out and screw them back

---

3 Available in the delightful Christmas novella, The Worst Noel in Kindle or paperback.

4 That was a plug for The Hellelujah Trail, available free on Smashwords. Guest starring the Dustpiggies by cartoonist Mike Bromage.

5 Fifty millennia, or twenty years before (infinity being relative), just over half of Britons' brains farted and they voted to leave the European Union, temporarily destabilizing the world economy. Americans, not to be outfarted, not only voted to leave America, but built a wall to keep out freeloaders and anyone who didn't speak "the native tongue." Since the voters were too lazy to define "native tongue" on the ballot, the courts ruled English was not a native tongue and turned the continent over to the few thousand original Americans who still spoke some semblance of theirs. The remaining former Americans were forced to immigrate to their countries of origin, who, it turned out, didn't want the obnoxious ungrateful bastards and turned them away. China and India opened their doors to the refugees, but immediately sold them into slavery and nobody wept a tear.

into place. "Would you, just once, name a punishment the rest of us can say before we run out breath?" She hit her temple with the heel of her hand to knock her eyeballs into place.

"I always prevail, dear sister."

Lucifer brushed the shoulders of his baby Moroccan seal shooting jacket. He watched from the corner of his eye. She sipped her drink. Hearing no further outbursts, he stepped back to the station.

"Pull."

Heston burst from the trap, arms and legs flailing as though he could flee through air. Lucifer choked up on his weapon, pulled the trigger in sync with the arc only to watch a shadow fall over the target.

An Imoogi skree shattered the sky. A wing dropped between his barrel and Heston's body, absorbing the brunt of the shot.

With a thump, a thud and a whomp the dragon crashed into the spectator arena. A snakelike tail whipped past Lucifer's ankles. Mephistopheles stabbed it with her cane, impaling it onto the back of yet another Vatican toady.

The Imoogi whipped and flailed on the shoreline, one arc-shaped wing bent at a right angle, unable to lift the creature into the sky. The former goddess Bast rested on her ass forty feet in front of Lucifer, dazed and concussed, her fingernails buried into Vatican cleric backs like cat's claws (the same Bast who, Lucifer professed only moments before, was closely supervising that pest Pilgrim). "Lucifer K. Morningstar," she shouted.

Lucifer slammed the shotgun into the dirt. "You ruined my shot."

"Your Most Vicious. How fortuit….." She caught her tongue in time. "How painful to see you again."

"You can say that again," one of the clerics mumbled, her nails buried six inches deep into his back.

Heston, believing he escaped the blast again, jumped to his feet and bounded down the beach. Lucifer fired from the hip. The shot ripped through Heston and carried him into the sea. His fist floated briefly above the surface, like the tip of Moses' staff, before flaming out in a black wisp of smoke.

Bast scrambled backwards in a crab walk, pulling herself by the fingernails. She wore a broad leather belt. A pouch dangled from her shoulder. "Wouldn't you like to hear my progress report?"

"Progress report?"

Mephistopheles balanced her cocktail on her cane seat.

"Progress report?"

Bast scrambled to her paws—back arched, ears alert, tail stiff and bristled.

People believe Bast resembles a cat because of the many Egyptian idols cast in the image of cats. In reality, she looks as human as any demon, god or demigod. Only the sharp-edged, elliptical face (called a "wedge head" on a cat) with a long angular nose and sharp-tipped ears, yellow almond eyes, long lean limbs with long nails, and fine hair covering most of her body resemble anything feline. And her long, chocolate-colored tail.

Lucifer stretched his neck and twisted it like a tornado. It wrapped Bast until his nose touched the tip of hers. His breath singed her cinnamon facial fur. "I didn't ask for progress, I ordered punishment. Pile driving punishment. Hammer pounding punishment pummeling him under layer after layer of thick, gooey asphalt steaming pain, then rolling over him with a steel-wheeled compacter to pop out his bones while he pleads for mercy he never receives."

Every hair on Bast's back stood straight. Lucifer relished her bowel-clinching terror, the once mighty Egyptian goddess, whose followers worshipped as the fiercest of feral creatures. Bast, goddess of jungle creatures who ripped men to shreds in seconds, whose yowls kept villages sleepless till sunrise, reduced in the modern consciousness to patron saint of cute purring cuddling kittens.

She batted him with her claws. They ripped his Monte Cristo jacket and broke on his scales. "Excuse me, Your Most Willing to Disembowel For the Slightest Provocation, but if that was your intention shouldn't you have sent him to a Hell of Heavy Equipment for Boys With Toys?"

Lucifer pinched Bast's neck, preparing to rip her spine, pelvis, tail, leg and foot bones through her throat and make them dance like marionettes over the lava waves.

Mephistopheles cleared her throat. She perched, legs crossed on her cane seat, nibbling on the habeñero garnish from her cocktail. "At least hear her out, big brother. How could it hurt?"

Lucifer froze, fingers opened in the Tiger's Claw Ninja Death Grip.

How could it hurt?

Lucifer knew she was goading him into a bad decision. Like the fall.[6]

---

6 The All Busy Body spent the better part of seven millennia mucking about with galaxies

He dropped Bast, crossed his arms and let the skepticism drip from his voice like pine resin. "I can't wait."

Bast scampered to her Imoogi. "We punished Pilgrim for three centuries." She reached under its wing and snapped the dislocated bone into place. "Fed him to griffins, torched him with dragons, ground him with sphinx teeth, and in every case...."

Lucifer knew the rest.

Pilgrim believed it "couldn't get worse than hell so he might as well enjoy it." He made friends with the beasts and probably unionized them. Lucifer once thought Pilgrim acted from dimwitted naivety, but deep in the lump of charcoal that should have been his heart he knew Pilgrim served as a perverse Super-Ego Über-Lucifer sent by His All Gotcha In the End.

"You should have seen it. The beasts fetched for him, rolled over, defended him when they thought we'd hurt him. We packed our gear to run and hide rather than face your wrath, but then Pilgrim explained what

---

and supernovas then decided, on the spur of the moment, to experiment with variable speeds of light. His "let the universe feel its way to a better reality" approach drove Lucifer nuts, especially since Lucifer cleaned up the messes He left in His wake.

"Can't you be consistent just once?" Lucifer asked.

The All Full of Himself puffed into a ringed emission nebula. "Geez O' Me, Morningstar? Could you do it better?"

Mephistopheles, who only recently discovered her breasts and spent half her time switching genders, whispered: "What are you waiting for? We're with you to a man."

"You bet I can," Lucifer told the All Muck It Up.

Next stop, this bunghole of creation, filled with ingrates and morons who blamed him for every poor choice they made.

a wonder… er… excruciatingly monstrous and perilous risk these creatures present."

Bast prostrated herself and then, seeing that the Imoogi hadn't moved, pulled a clicker from her belt and snapped it. The Imoogi joined her in the same prostrate position. "Pilgrim explained that we'd never truly punish resistant souls with insidious creatures from their id until the insidious creatures first surrendered their hearts and souls to us."

Lucifer drummed his nails on his forearms. Failing to create the effect he intended, he drummed his toe claws on the clerics backs. The clerics yelped up and down the scale.

Bast rolled the dragon onto his back. "Watch." She stretched her claws and kneaded its belly like bread. His legs stretched in ecstasy, puffs of contented smoke rising from his nostrils.

A fissure formed between Lucifer's parietal and occipital bones. His brain squeezed through. Not much, just enough to paint the cracks.

"Is that dragon happy?"

Bast rubbed a paw behind her ear. "A reward system works better at this stage, especially since his wing still hurts." She emptied her bag and laid out a maze of uneven hoops, ladders, trapezes and platforms.

"We call this an agility course." She grabbed a handful of fingers from her pocket and tossed one to the dragon. She let him crunch the bone then led him to the beginning of the course.

Lucifer's fissure opened wider. His brain explored the outer surface to see if an outdoor party might be fun.

Bast clicked. The dragon flew through the first three hoops. She tossed a finger and pointed to the ladder. The Imoogi snapped up the finger then climbed each rung and somersaulted to the trapeze.

"Pilgrim can train any nightmare the prisoners conjure. Blue-tipped Diamond Dragons to make most recalcitrant miscreant scream, chemically-enhanced Chimera Choirs, Tantric Torture Tarantulas. We've found more freedom to express ourselves creatively through chaos and mayhem than ever."

The Imoogi sailed through every hoop, climbed every platform, hopped every trapeze and every rung of every ladder in spite of his dislocated wing. At each stage Bast rewarded him with a finger from her pocket and spurred him on with a click.

After the finale, a quadruple somersault through parallel hoops with a wand shooting fireworks in his teeth, Bast approached Lucifer with a thick dot-matrix spreadsheet print-out. "That's not even the be... most horrific part. Pilgrim taught us how to train the beasts, how to market them and even how to set up the databases and accounts. We get custom orders from the farthest regions of hell. Our budget's in the black for the first time since you created our department."

She held out the spreadsheet, trying to hide the pride on her face. She tucked her chin into her neck and bowed as she held forth her treasure like the tribute of a conquered empire.

Lucifer's left horn popped its socket and soared like an unguided missile, ripping through the storm troopers and blasting the loading docks at the far end of the island. The sky filled with smoke, debris and pterodactyl shrieks. His right horn sailed across the ocean to blow away a bus of civilians on their way to work at one of Hell's many mind-numbing office complexes where the damned repeated the same task eternally for the generous reward of carpal tunnel syndrome.

He beat Bast's head repeatedly with the mangled Paperazzi until nothing remained above her shoulders but the C3 vertebrae. The printouts flew from her claws. "You're not supposed to run in the black, you ignorant, inconsequential, speaking when not spoken to about-to-be-demoted moron. You're supposed to live in perpetual fear that your department, your rationale and your entire existence are on the chopping block."

"Not to mention you hate pets," Mephistopheles added, thumbing through the printouts as though checking the line item of every expense. This only inflamed Lucifer's fury even more.

"I especially hate pets."

Lucifer's tail ripped through his pants and lashed at Bast's backside and shoulders. "I hate puppies and goldfish, talking parrots that say, 'Polly wanna cracker.' I hate turtles, gerbils and guinea pigs. I hate sitting on furniture covered with pet hair and stepping in puppy poo and dogs wagging their tails with their tongues hanging out, and looking at pet videos on YouTube and Facebook...."

"Don't forget kittens," Mephistopheles added, jotting a note on the printout.

Lucifer's two remaining horns blasted into the stratosphere, upward through the ocean and landed on a beach in East Los Angeles where they appeared on an episode of Unexplained Mysteries. "I especially hate kittens. I hate people fawning over kittens, and kitten videos, and the smell of litter boxes and the feel of tiny little kitten claws when they grab your fingers..." He grabbed Bast by her T-6 vertebrae for a face-to-spinal cord chat.

"You aren't breeding kittens are you?"

Nothing raised Lucifer's ire more than the thought of kittens. Kittens and Pilgrim. Kittens and Pilgrim and the thought that Bast brought the two of them together.

From that tiny seed, those two images juxtaposed, those two seemingly innocent images (at least to the world at large, a world filled with innocence, a world that didn't understand the devious inner mind of a Deity who could fill the world with mewling, purring, kneading, pawing, pulling at your furniture, big-eyed, all-fucking-filled-with-innocence-and-then-hawking-up-shit-and-furballs-just-like-Pilgrim kittens), from those two images juxtaposed bloomed a garden of invective, malediction, curses and swear words that turned right into the world of humans with an undersea mega thrust earthquake magnitude of 9.0 causing a 133 foot tsunami that traveled six miles into Japan's interior, flooded a nuclear reactor and shifted the earth ten inches on its axis.

Yes, the earth moved. Even in Hell.

Mephistopheles sighed, dropped the printout to her side and gripped His Satanic Majesty by the shoulder. The semi-spineless Bast scrabbled away like a two-legged crab and cowered underneath her Imoogi.

"Overreact much?"

Lucifer stormed off the range, leaving footprints six to seven inches deep in the backs of clerics who'd been whining for millennia that they couldn't see any harm in dispensing dispensations for a few pointless pennies.

He reached the loading dock only to discover the pile of debris blasted by his horn was his armored sleigh and the bodies of his eight ferocious pterodactyls,[7] or, rather, their scattered wings, beaks and limbs.

Mephistopheles offered her cane chair. "I'd suggest you learn to control your temper, but it's half your charm and you'd only unleash the other half on me."

He wouldn't even glance sideways. He said under his breath, so she could just hear it. "Have the storm troopers make a raft from the clerics. And dispatch Bast and Pilgrim to my office."

And then, loud enough to be heard clearly: "At least I win. 25-24."

One simple task. How hard is that?

Beginning a meeting with "Jesus H. Christ," the single most forbidden phrase in hell, bodes badly for the remaining agenda.

In Bast's defense (for which, in hell, there is none), Lucifer invited her to sit at the far end of his snow leopard couch. His manservant Struggles, who currently took the form of a platypus,[8] waddled past on the fiberglass carpet in his bare feet, balancing a sterling silver tray

---

7 Formerly known as Smasher, Bouncer, Basher and Vixen (she was as naughty a girl in hell as was her alter ego at the North Pole), Dammit, Druid, Thunderhead and Blitzkrieg.

8 Lucifer transformed Struggles, his long suffering manservant, into a beast of burden, prey or even ridicule whenever it tickled his fancy, which proved damned inconvenient to Struggles' trade, not to mention his tailor.

on webbed paws. He stepped on the leopard's tail, the leopard swiped Bast's entire left side (exactly as Lucifer intended), Bast leaped four feet into the air and swore, "Jesus H. Christ."

She immediately fell onto her face into the scratchy fibers. She kowtowed for mercy even while the rash spread across her body. Struggles regained his balance only by grabbing the baby Jesus' penis on Lucifer's new installation of Michelangelo's Pied-a-terre.[9] He dropped the tray on Lucifer's desk and dashed through the exit behind bookshelves bearing the archives of lost Gnostic Heretics, third through fifth century AD.[10]

Advantage Lucifer.

Mephistopheles screwed a member of parliament into his cigarette holder and fired his lighter fueled by British Oil executives. He wore Christian Dior, who complained every time he adjusted position that he could have achieved a better line with a tailored outfit and not someone straight off the rack.[11] "Really, Lucifer, who are you showing off for?"

On a better day, one in which his temper didn't wipe out coastal Japan, he might have recalled that he sent Pilgrim topside to interfere with human destinies before. That visit ended in monumental disaster—thousands of souls saved from eternal perdition, and three million souls who would have been tobacco addicts spared the

---

9 If this strikes readers as another subtle plug for my novel, Raising Hell, it most certainly would be.

10 Bound in their skin with faces on the spines for easy reference.

11 Unfortunately, Mephistopheles was in a hurry and couldn't wait for the torturers to restore Dior after stretching him an additional six inches on the rack.

ravages of lung cancer. The only soul to earn a ticket to hell would have done so anyway.[12]

Lucifer convinced himself he wouldn't repeat the mistake this time.[13]

Lucifer buttered his leatherback sea turtle scone with Javan rhinoceros jam and poured a cup of Rafflesia flower tea. Lord Byron,[14] his personal secretary reached for a scone and Lucifer batted him away. Byron scampered to the end of the desk to take notes for the meeting and hissed with his fingers, but only when he thought Lucifer was looking away.

"Don't be mean on my account," Pilgrim said. "I'm the one you want to punish." Pilgrim sat in lotus position in front of the desk in the middle of the carpet, still wearing the scratchy woolen monk's robe assigned to him in the Hell of His Own Making, the kind woven to keep the skin red and raw to remind the wearer to be penitent.

"I punish everyone. Unfortunately, my sibling persuaded me to send you on assignment against my better judgment."

Mephistopheles looked up from his glass. "I did what?"

Lucifer rapped Mephistopheles on the noggin with his curcifix.[15]

---

12 If this strikes readers as another subtle plug for my novel, Raising Hell, it most certainly would be.

13 The currents of denial flow through every channel of creation—deep, clear and convenient, which is what makes them so easy to ignore, even for Supreme Lords of Hell.

14 Lord Byron, Lucifer's personal secretary, spent eternity reduced to roaming Lucifer's desk as nothing but a hand. Having written that he'd rather rule in hell than serve on earth, he got the worst end of both bargains.

15 A golden shepherd's staff with middle finger extended.

Pilgrim adjusted the hem of his robe, causing Lucifer to turn his head away. "Last time you hated the results."

Lucifer drummed his nails. Byron drummed his nails in time. Lucifer rapped Byron's knuckles. "This time I'm putting you under Bast's direct supervision. Since you two work so well together."

Bast raised her head, her yellow eyes bigger than the kittens in Margaret Keane knock-off posters. "Training dragons is one thing. But not this, Your Most Willing to Degrade, Humiliate and Denigrate. Send me to The Hell of A Million Paper Cuts Doused With Iodine and Rolled in Table Salt. Send me to The Hell of Catering to an Endless Line of Leering, Pinching and Insinuating Buffoons With a Million Hands Each and Nowhere to Put Them But My Body and the Sense of Humor of a Nine-Year-Old but the Hygiene of a Six-Year-Old. But please don't send me on a personal mission."

"So glad you volunteered." Lucifer snapped his fingers and Byron spread open a folder with photos. "Meet Kansas Senator Carly Anne Baronbottom. She'll maneuver a gun control bill through the US Congress for the first time in forever. That's bad for hell's business. Turn her into a cat lady. The ultimate cat lady."

Mephistopheles pulled an emery board from his inside jacket pocket and buffed his tuxedo black nails. "Maybe she wouldn't have passed the bill if we hadn't used those gun rights advocates as skeet targets."

Lucifer poked the tiger with the curcifix, who ripped the leg of her Christian Dior, and hers as well. "Fill her house with tabbies, torties and domestic shorthairs. Fill her closets with litter boxes, her cabinets, even her showers. I want cat shit in her bedroom, bathroom and under the refrigerator door. I want her to stumble over empty cat food cans and trip over cat toys. Her house should stink of so much cat urine the mailman leaves her mail seven houses down. I want her only thought of the Senate to be a place she writes to campaign for animal welfare rights."

Bast dug her nails into her forehead. "This is my thanks?" She curled into a ball. "We turn uncontrollable torture beasts into efficient, profitable cruelty machines and you piss away my goddess powers on a politician?"

Mephistopheles kicked her with a toe. "Look on the bright side. All expenses paid vacation. Time topside. Streaming cat videos."

Bast peeked up from the carpet, ass raised high, one eye under her arm in an impossible contortion. "What's a cat video?"

Lucifer dug his nails into his desk. "Disgusting things. Cloying cute motion pictures of kittens playing and knocking things off shelves. You'll want to hurl your lunch and every lunch you've ever eaten. Even the long digested bones of brain-dead box trolls."

Bast threw herself face forward into the fiberglass. "Please, Lord Lucifer, I'll lick the toes of leprous leprechauns. I'll launder the long johns of incontinent lounge lizards. Anything but time topside with Pilgrim and Cat Videos."

Lucifer kicked his desk over, sending Byron crawling into the interior drawers for safety. It leveled Pilgrim under its weight, flattening him like a corn tortilla in the sun of the Sonoran desert. "Enough of your bellyaching. You and Pilgrim leave at once."

"Don't you want me to sign a contract?" Pilgrim asked, peering upward through the desk's under frame.

The pressure built at the seam of his skull again, as though his head was a cherry-red hive about to blossom on the surface of his neck. The last time he made Pilgrim sign a contract it went so far south he felt like he was cornered by confederate rednecks with half their teeth and every one demanding he marry their sisters and cousins.

"No contract. You're on your honor."

He rapped his curcifix three times and swept from the room, leaving them to shudder in awe at his departure. Even as his Demonic Presence departed in a dark cloud of smoke, however, he thought, just for an instant, that he saw that devious beast Bast smiling.

In which all's well that ends at all

Lucifer and Mephistopheles toured the Seventh Circle on his land yacht, The Frying Dutchmen, built from tyrannosaurus ribs and dragon scales with pterodactyl wings for sails.[16] They relaxed on seats upholstered with the skins of baby Saimaa ringed seals.

Lucifer leaned over the bow sporting his naval blue broad coat with Jabot collar, and knee britches. His tail wrapped around the boat railing and he curled his clawed toes into his fine monk leather shoes, the monks complaining each time he curled them. He held his bi-corne hat out over the rail, gripping the corners with both hands.

Mephistopheles wore a Siberian tiger bikini that barely covered two of her six breasts. A St. Lucia racer snake sandal dangled from her toe as she stirred her diesel and Chinati Vergano martini with dapne berries.

---

16 Still attached to the pterodactyls

"Do you ever think that each time you send Pilgrim on a new assignment, you set yourself up for failure?"

Lucifer ripped his bi-corne hat to shreds. When he realized Mephistopheles didn't see him do it, he conveniently dropped the pieces over the side. "Absolutely not. This time, instead of concocting a grand scheme to entrap him I gave him one tiny, evil task." He turned to face her, dangling his tail over the side so he could swat any passersby. "With all the effort I've invested so far I have to believe there's some small…."

"Cause for hope?"

Her words, mimicking exactly what he intended to say, caught in his throat like WildEye Mullet shark bait, the hook sinking into his uvula and refusing to turn loose until he confronted the irony, the outright wrongness, the utter blasphemy of speaking the words "cause for hope."

Mephistopheles, who'd taken up jazz dancing, sprang across the deck in a practiced coffee grinder step.[17] She leaned against the bow and squeezed his hand in a gesture of camaraderie that, at any other moment, would have earned her a ticket to the Hell of Violators of Personal Space Where the Rest of Eternity is Shared With Family Members, Co-Workers and Exes Who Assume Every Aspect of Your Life Is Theirs to Explore, Share, Compare and Post on Social Media. "That's the dilemma with your pest Pilgrim. Everything he does gives cause for hope, which in our

---

17 A full turn followed by a whipped turn, but the dancer squats and jumps mid-turn then follows with a full circle around the body with the free leg and the supporting leg hops over the circling leg. If the dancer doesn't collapse, everyone gets super-hyped, or wonders what the hell the world of dance is coming to.

domain is an unmitigated, unparalleled, unqualifiedly complete catastrophe."

His iPhone rang. He snatched it from his broad coat pocket like fissionable material in meltdown. "I never permitted iPhones."

Mephistopheles pulled her iPhone 9s- from her bikini top. "Pilgrim diverted a shipment that Amazon. com lost to computer error. Wasn't even stealing. According to Apple it never existed."

Lucifer smashed the offending object to tiny bits. He stomped on the tiny bits for good measure.

"No problem. The text cc'd to me." She scrolled her SMS app. "They're back. Pilgrim diverted the yacht to your office."

In that instant they crashed into the Capitol Complex for the Diabolical Administration of Perpetual Pain and Punishment Accompanied by a Simultaneous Inescapable Sense of Dejá Vu. The mast smashed through the lobby window and impaled a receptionist. The anchor dropped, crushing two employees on their cigarette break.

Pilgrim shouted, "Hello," from several hundred feet below.

Lucifer looked over the bow. Pilgrim waved his bi-corne hat. "Look what floated by in the wind, sir. The pieces anyway. It isn't as pretty as it used to be, but I think it will fit just as well."

Lucifer scaled down the anchor rope and snatched the hat from Pilgrim's fat little fingers. "No one asked you to fix this."

"It was the Christian thing to do."

Lucifer beat Pilgrim with the hat until nothing remained but the duck feather that once tucked into the brim.

Pilgrim remained as round as ever, but flattened to a pancake on the acid rain asphalt. Not satisfied, Lucifer stomped on him to flatten him even more, until he looked like a round paper dot lying on the ground.

"Are you finished?" Mephistopheles asked. She draped a cape of California Condor feathers over her shoulders and replaced her sandals with Blanding's Turtle skin boots.

"No, but I don't feel like sending him back to the Spanish Inquisition for heretic practice anymore." He marched into the complex, leaving it to Pilgrim to waddle in under his own power.

The doorman spotted Lucifer and leaped twelve feet above the frame. Since Lucifer usually entered the capitol complex from the bottom floor, the sight of His Satanic Majesty not only sent him into total panic, he redecorated the wall a new shade of chocolate with the refuse from his backside.

A former lead singer for Black Sabbath, who once boasted of his relationship with Satan on stage, shouted, "It's Lucifer. He's coming this way." Every soul in the hallway scrambled up the walls, down the halls, over each other's backs, on each other's heads and in each other's ears.

Lucifer ripped off his broad coat, flinging it over his head. Struggles leaped from an office doorway to catch it before it hit the floor. Pilgrim, with two knees extended from his flattened body, bumped through the doors before they slammed back on him.

"Don't you want to know how we did?"

"I'm sure your little Senator saved the world." Lucifer kicked an accountant who failed to make it out of the dog pile. He bounced off the elevator doors at the far end of the hall, sideways and up the adjoining stairs.

Lucifer shook off his knee breeches, forcing Struggles to dive to his ankles to catch them. He successfully avoided tripping Lucifer, but became tangled in the clothes and rolled like a ball of laundry down the length of the hall.

"Typical Lucifer," Bast said, "only interested when it's convenient for you." She rested her shoulder against an office door. Her vinyl dominatrix suit included a headpiece cut with kitty ears. Her leather whip coiled in her right hand, waiting to strike, and her tail curled up and over her shoulder.

Mephistopheles hooked her elbow though his. "Bast has a point." She screwed a forgotten sixteenth century pope into her cigarette holder then dragged her fore nail up Lucifer's chest to ignite it. "You can be such an ass at times." The pope screamed as his forehead flared.

Pilgrim's hips popped from his knees so that he remained flattened only from the waist up. He hopped around like a wind up toy. "Wait'll you hear how." Lucifer wondered where his voice came from. "We send an email asking her office to sponsor a pet adoption day."

Bast polished her nails against her vinyl suit. "Where people bring foster pets to stores for people to adopt. The suckers can't resist a fur ball in their hands. They cart them home without thinking about pee stains and chewed shoes."

An arm popped out of Pilgrim's fly. "See? She makes it sound diabolical. The way you'd like." Five fingers blossomed from the arm and a hand followed behind. They felt their way around Pilgrim's belt loop.

"She meets a famous female mystery writer who adopts two kittens. They start dating. Who would've guessed? But because the Senator's from Kansas…"

"Reddest of the Red states," Bast added. She lashed her whip and cracked it along the bare floor. The floor, tiled with 20th century Darwinists, yelped with pain.

Pilgrim discovered his other arm in his hip pocket. "The Senator's scared to profess their love in public. So the writer dumps her."

Bast pulled the lash back like a fishing line. "Her next mystery featured a Gay Kansas Senator who fosters pets and murders her lover. Number One bestseller."

The elevator doors opened. The operator, caught playing a Nintendo game, dropped it through the grate in sheer panic and peed himself completely onto the carpet, leaving nothing but a puddle and his uniform.

Lucifer waited for everyone to cram inside. When the doors closed he announced, "British Invasion, Struggles." Still bundled hopelessly in nautical laundry, Struggles managed to extract a tie-dyed shirt, bell-bottomed jeans and leather boots with five-inch heels.

Pilgrim's hands explored his waistline looking for more of his body. "Now she's in a deep funk. She ignores her staff's advice and focuses only on animal rights. Opens her own shelter and takes in hundreds of cats. It becomes the model for cat shelters across the country."

Lucifer reached into Struggle's clothes bundle and snatched a 1958 Tobacco Sunburst Stressed Paul.[18] He plugged it into his skull, cranked it to 1100, and launched into the solo from Whole Lotta Love Sucks.

18 Complete with stressed Les's face peering out from the headstock between the tuning keys.

90

His botched chords and frayed notes shattered the ear drums and splintered the nerves of everyone in the three by six by four elevator.

When the doors opened to the bottom floor, no cheering, adoring audience waited to applaud him. Lucifer kicked the frames so that the doors would no longer shut.

During the long, march down the vacant hall Pilgrim filled the vacuum with prattle about Baronbottom's cat shelters and cat causes. "You'll appreciate this, sir. After she dies, the Senate passes a resolution declaring her, 'The Ultimate Cat Lady.'"

They reached Lucifer's reception desk. His ornate office doors featured panel after panel of penitent souls devoured, disemboweled, drawn and quartered, and boiled in oil just for seeking an audience. Pilgrim's hands gripped his shoulders and lifted them from his waistline. He looked like a headless troll.

With one last strenuous tug, Pilgrim popped his head, and then his stomach into place. "Isn't that what you wanted, Your Most Ungracious? To make her the ultimate cat lady?"

Did Bast purr? Mephistopheles climbed onto the reception desk and executed a hip walk, followed by a fan kick. "You have to admit, big brother, that's exactly what you asked for."

Lucifer raised the guitar to smash it across Pilgrim's eager, earnest, approval anticipating mug. Only at the last minute did he think the better of it. Not damaging Pilgrim, of course, but his one-of-a-kind 1958 Tobacco Sunburst Stressed Paul.

"If your mission was so successful, where is she?" Bast coiled her whip.

"We had a slight hiccup." Pilgrim held up two fingers to display almost no space between them.

The steam in Lucifer's skull rose to a boil. "A hiccup?"

"An escape clause." Pilgrim squeezed his fists, lips and beady little eyes in unison as if to make himself the smallest target possible. "If you care for the least of Go…, er, His Most To Never Be Spoken Of's creatures, you earn a free trip upstairs."

Lucifer's Stressed Paul burst at every seam. Stressed Les bolted from the headstock and ran for the hills. The pressure in Lucifer's skull popped an eyeball from its socket releasing a gale force of hot steam that melted the new Gharial crocodile tiles decorating the hallways (and the Gharial crocodiles wearing them).

Lucifer forced the vowel sounds over the escaping steam from his eye socket. "The downstairs trip was the end game."

Pilgrim lowered his eyes, like a child with his hand in the cookie jar. "You should have written that in the contract."

Lucifer clinched his fists like boxing gloves. "What contract?"

Bast cleared her throat. "The contract he offered to sign." She rubbed her back against a door frame, winding and unwinding her whip.

Mephistopheles chewed the side of a nail. "I distinctly recall his offer." Lucifer's glare pinned her to the wall like a high speed harpoon.

Bast backed one foot against the wall. "Might as well bring up the other thing."

Her words struck Lucifer like ice at the base of his spine. Ice, a sensation never felt in hell, never imagined in hell. Like round squares, inconceivable until this moment. He slowly swiveled his gaze to Pilgrim, leveling it like the sight on a 700 caliber gun. "What other thing?"

Pilgrim turned his toes inward and stuck a finger between his teeth. "A small thing really, considered the size of hell. Infinite, room for everything and everyone."

"Go on." Lucifer stretched the sound to increase the menace. "Goo oonn."

"She left her cats. Hundreds of cats. No one wanted responsibility."

Lucifer pictured himself looking through a telescope at another Lucifer looking through a telescope at another Lucifer in another hell in another universe a million dimensions away.

"Gggoooo oooonnnn."

"Better see for yourself," Bast said. Without waiting for proper protocol, which called for storm troopers to open his office doors with pomp, ceremony and more brimstone than the explosion of Krakatoa, she yanked them open and gestured through the entry.

A foul and funky fetor, akin to the stench of a hundred winos packed into a broom closet, barreled down the hallway. They held their noses, trying not to heave.

Wait! Did he know that stench?

Please, no and let it never be.

The sound of cats meowing, screeching and caterwauling, confirmed his fears.

He smelled litter boxes. Not one, not two, but dozens upon dozens. A smell he recognized only because he personally designed the litter box torture for the cat phobic Benito Mussolini.

He shouted without thinking, "I hate cats." His entire body bloomed red. Red hot fire and pumping blood red, not the candy apple red that artists painted him. He couldn't believe he lost control in front of his minions so easily. Deep down he realized he knew how to torture Mussolini only because he hated cats even more.

He shoved Bast aside and tore into his office.

Cats everywhere.

Cats on bookshelves, cats on the mantle, cats on his desk, cats hanging from the chandelier, cats kneading his carpet, cats climbing his bat skin curtains.

He stepped over a blue point Siamese and found the remains of Michaelangelo's Pied-a-Terre. The sculpture lay in a dozen pieces covered in cat feces, regurgitated Little Friskies cat food and hair balls.

His entire bookcase of Alternative Gospels lay upturned on the floor, now home to a nest of domestic Orientals with their boxy ears and fierce yowls. The Gospel of Pilate, which claimed Jesus bribed Pilate to switch places with Barabbas, lay open and torn to shreds. The cover to The Gospel of Martha, which claimed Mary Magdalene slept with anyone who would write her into their gospel, lay with its pages shredded on the other side of the room. A green and runny hair ball covered The Gospel of Doubting Thomas, which claimed Jesus hid in his grave until the disciples forced him to come out and then he ran away so they wouldn't turn him in for a reward.

"This is a temporary solution until we find homes for them, of course," Pilgrim said. "You might even be able to negotiate something with…" he lowered his voice to his whisper "…He Who Shall Not Be Named." He sat on the corner of the desk and picked up a flame point Ragdoll, who went limp in his lap. "I don't mean Lord Voldemort, of course, I mean…." He pointed his finger upward.

Lucifer grabbed his curcifix and swept Pilgrim, the cats, his laptop and everything else from the surface. "Clear these infernal beasts out of my office. I will never, ever, at any time in eternity, allow pets, especially not cats, in hell."

He leaped over the desk and battered Pilgrim about the skull and shoulders. "Not cats, not kittens, not cuddly creatures with names like 'Mittens.' Nothing that yowls, nothing that meows, nothing that leaves the house at night to prowl. Get them out now, I don't care how, or I will slice and dice and disembowel."

For once they got the message. Even his slacker sibling Mephistopheles. They scrambled about his office stuffing scratching, hissing and clawing cats under their armpits, in their pants and even cradling them under their necks. Within a year (which is really nothing in eternity), they removed every feline presence from his office.

When they left for good, and Lucifer had a moment alone for the first time in millennia, he relaxed behind his desk with a cup of Texas Wild Rice tea and Kakapo sandwiches. Donald Trump and Ted Cruz roasted in the fireplace cursing each other for ruining the American Republican Party.

Something scratched inside his pen drawer. He opened it slightly and peeked inside. A calico tabby, barely two months old hopped into his lap.

"Struggles," he shouted at full voice. Instead of fleeing in terror, the creature grabbed his pinky and batted at his fingers. He couldn't resist poking its fat little belly. A purr as loud as a Caterpillar excavator filled his office, drowning out the petty Republican bickering in his fireplace.

The kitten leaped on his shoulder and rubbed his cheek.

Struggles appeared wearing a freshly starched collar, which made it impossible to turn his neck, or walk comfortably (an item Lucifer insisted he wear at all times). "Would you like me to toss it in the fire, Your Most Unholy."

Lucifer reached up to grab the kitten, but it curled around his neck and fell asleep, purring louder than before. "No," he said. He scratched the kitten behind its ears without thinking. "Perhaps, just once, we can make an exception."

Phillip T. Stephens' parents found him behind a headstone while necking in a grave yard on Halloween. Turning up with an infant so scandalized their Baptist families that they married within the week. The newlyweds were so poor, the made the infant author sleep in a carved out Jack-o-lantern until his fourth birthday, feeding him pumpkin milk instead of formula and pumpkin seeds for cereal.

The semi-literate Stephens painted his first story on the kitchen wall, a crude drawing in fecal matter that depicted his mother beating his father to death with the family Bible. The incident never happened, but the toddler expressed his mother's inner rage at his minister father so well, the family immediately recognized his destiny as a story-teller. They spanked him anyway.

As would his school teachers, Sunday School teachers, principals, grandparents, aunts and uncles. Nonetheless, as he cried himself to sleep in his dog bed in the closet the night of his punishment, the young author heard his parents and family laughing over his latest outrageous escapade. Which is why, years later, after failing as Kentucky Fried Chicken clerk, Kerbey Vacuum salesman, cigarette phone salesman for Scientology and lawn maintenance engineer, Stephens finally started writing.

He currently rescues cats with his wife Carol for Austin Siamese Rescue. His also wrote the novels Raising Hell and its follow up The Worst Noel, Cigerets, Guns & Beer and Seeing Jesus.

Seagulls
By Rayne Hall

The birds looked so harmless.

While the stencils dried above the dado rail, Josie squatted on the carpet, eating her first breakfast in the new studio flat.

Three seagulls stood outside the window, white-feathered and silver-winged, their eyes yellow halos around death-dark cores. Every time Josie lifted a spoonful of muesli to her mouth, their greedy stares followed her hand.

According to the Welcome To Sussex pamphlet, European herring gulls were an endangered species, worthy of protection. On the brochure's cover, seagulls looked so pretty: white-feathered, silver-tipped, soaring serenely in an azure sky.

In close-up reality, they were ugly, unromantic beasts, from the wrinkled flat clawed feet and the grey-pink legs to the folded wings ending in feathers like black blades. Each thumb-long beak had a hole in the upper half, some weird kind of nose she supposed, a gap through which she could see the misty sky. Then there was the red, a splash of scarlet on each beak, as if they carried fresh innards from a slaughter feast.

A sudden screech, and they dropped their pretence at peacefulness. Big beaks were pecking at her miniature roses, ripping them out and apart, tossing green fragments.

Josie stormed to the window, waving the tea towel like a weapon. Three pairs of wings unfolded, filled the window, lifted off. Screeches of outrage tailed off into the distance.

Of the pretty pink roses she had planted with so much care yesterday, only stems and shreds remained. With delicate fingers and tender words, she pressed the roots back into the soil and gave them water to settle back in.

She returned to work, sponging the next layer of stencils, delicate blooms in pink which would go well with chiffon curtains.

#

At noon, she left the stencils to dry and prepared lunch — muesli again, since she had not had time to stock her cupboard.

The gulls were back. Sharp bills pointed at the muesli on her spoon, begrudging her every bite. The one with deep grooves on its chin knocked its beak against the window. Tap-tap, tap-tap. more fiercely: klacketeklacketeckackateklack.

The oat-flakes stuck dry in Josie's throat.

The tallest of the gulls, with head feathers standing up like a punk's haircut, tilted its head back and trumpeted a shattering scream. Kreeeeee! Kreeeee! The white chest vibrated with screeches which could have brought down the walls of Jericho. Josie wasn't sure if the window glass trembled, but the shudders in her spine were real.

The gull closest to her had obscene red stains on its beak, like a vampire's bloodied lips. Josie tried not to look, but she had to. Their closeness sent chills up her back, even with the transparent safety of double-glazing shielding her from predatory beaks.

If only she had curtains in place, preferably something as thick and solid as the garish seventies drapes she'd left behind in the shared London flat.

The red-billed gull unfolded its wings, increasing its size to fill the large frame, and more. Josie ducked behind two unpacked suitcases, but still their stares followed her. The studio flat, which had appeared so spacious when she had first viewed it, now closed in on her.

Living by the sea had seemed such a good idea, especially in St Leonards, where the streets hummed with history. She had pictured herself in a dress of sprigged muslin, strolling along the promenade on the arm of a Mr Darcy. A grey bombazine gown and a Mr Rochester would be good, too.

The gulls clucked like hens, trumpeted like elephants, screamed like pigs at slaughter, the noise shrilling through the window-glass and echoing in the unfurnished room. Why had they sought her out?

She scanned the houses on the other side of the road, Regency terraces with elegant wrought-iron balconies and bow windows on pale, ornamented façades. No unwanted visitors plagued those windows, although some seagulls socialised on distant roof gables and chimney pots.

Josie thought of squirting them with water from the plant mist spray, but living in cliffs, gulls were used to splashes, and of pelting them with hazelnuts from the muesli box, but they might just let the missiles drop off their feathers and gobble up the food.

Resolutely, she pulled her floaty velvet coat from a suitcase and threw it full force against the window. The big gull stepped back and dropped off the ledge, but within moments it was back.

Josie retreated to the windowless bathroom, where she emptied a jar of perfumed crystals, a farewell gift from her flatmates, into the steaming tub. Like always, the scent of lavender soothed her. During the hot soak, she was able to view the seagulls' behaviour as a mere annoyance, and her own reaction as ridiculous.

How strange that the birds homed in on her, and how strange that she was so frightened of them. After all, they were only birds, kept out by a double panel of solid glass.

But then, she'd always been frightened easily. As a child, she feared the neighbour's dogs, just because they were big and fierce looking, while young children patted them with fond trust. She could not bring herself to go near the farmer's cows, or the ugly looking turkeys in the cage. All harmless animals, of course, and only a stupid child would be afraid of them. The other kids made fun of Josie's fears, teasing her without mercy until she despised herself.

She covered her legs in thick soapy foam and shaved them with deliberate slow strokes, a reassuring routine, and stayed in the bath until she had used up all the boiler's hot water.

By the time she had rubbed her skin dry, the gulls had departed, probably to the beach to snatch snacks from unsuspecting tourists. In the bright sun, the glass showed zigzagging white lines where beaks dribbled, and white faeces gleamed on the windowsill ledge.

With the monsters gone, she browsed the mail order catalogue for curtains and furniture, designing a light-filled, romantic space with swathes of chiffon and Regency prints, and pondered what to wear when she started her new job on Monday.

During supper — more muesli — the same three gulls returned. Klacklack klackeklack. All three, hammering against the glass. Josie recognized the grooved throat, the blood-stained beak, the punk-style feathered head.

They knocked the window by moving their heads forward and back. Even ghastlier, the small one kept the tip of its upper beak glued to the glass, and vibrated the lower one. The whole pane rattled in an angry staccato. Josie had heard that bridges collapsed when a unit of soldiers marched in synchronised steps. Would the window break under the persistent pecking?

For the first time, she wished she was still in London, in the soulless grey tower block with views of other soulless grey tower blocks, in a flat furnished with someone's hideous nineteen-eighties leftovers, with flatmates whose unwashed dishes stank up the kitchen and whose stereos thumped through the night. The flatmates would know what to do, or would at any rate drown out her fears with their loud laughter and roaring rap.

"Oh, go away, go away!" she shouted at the beasts. Without the slightest shift of a leg, blink of an eye, twitch of a wing, they sat and stared.

She grabbed a fistful of muesli. "If I give you this,

will you go?"

Kreeee-kreeeeeee. Kreeee. Impatient foot-tapping, as if they knew what was in the box.

She turned the squeaking handle, tilted the window, and dropped the muesli on the sill. They snatched the crumbs as soon as they fell, three scimitar-sharp beaks devouring the raisins and oat-flakes faster than she could dip her hand back into the box. Kreee-kreee.

If she gave them enough to fill their stomach, they would not bother hanging around. She grabbed another fistful and pushed her hand through the gap.

Pain shot like a piercing nail through her flesh.

She pulled her hand back, slammed the window shut and twisted the lock. Dark red blood streamed from the wound, dripping thick blotches on the pristine white windowsill.

The gulls yelled in angry triumph.

Having neither antiseptic nor a first aid kit, Josie rinsed her hand under the tap and wrapped it with an embroidered handkerchief. She needed allies, someone who had experienced this kind of harassment and knew what to do. But she had not yet introduced herself to her neighbours, and the harridan in the flat below had complained about the noise of Josie dragging suitcases up the stairs.

Dusk descended, but the gulls did not retire to roost.

Klackedekackedeklcackedeklack, they hammered at the window. Josie blessed the double glazing. Even if they cracked one pane, the second would resist, wouldn't it?

Josie scanned the other buildings in the evening mist. No seagulls were attacking the mock-Georgian retirement homes, the Victorian gothics, the concrete monstrosities from the seventies. Why had they picked her?

Maybe because she was at home when most residents were out at work. Maybe the absence of net curtains had lured them with a tempting view inside. Maybe they'd tried all the other windows, and learnt that they'd not get fodder there. She cursed her weakness of giving them muesli. Now they would not go away.

A soft, prolonged scratch. And another.

One gull was scratching along the edge of the window; the other two pecked at the putty that held the glass in the wooden frame. Josie had heard that great-tits and other songbirds sometimes nibbled at window-frame putty because they loved the flavour of the linseed oil it contained. Since seagulls didn't eat putty, what was their plan? If they pecked the stuff to loosen the glass from its frame, she would be trapped in a room with three violent seagulls hacking their beaks at her. What then?

Klackedeklack.

With her pulse thumping in her throat and ears, Josie put her door on the latch, and tried the flat next to hers, and the ones above, but nobody replied. The flats on the ground and first floors were still unoccupied after refurbishment. That left the one on the floor below.

Josie knocked and waited. A toilet flushed inside. At last, the door squealed open. "You." The sharp-nosed woman, with grey hair clinging like a steel helmet to her skull, stabbed a finger at Josie. "Do you know what the time is?"

"I, ahem…I know it's late, but..."

"Nine o'clock. Nine o'clock, do you hear?" Her voice whined like a dentist's drill, shrill, painful, persistent. "A time when decent people expect to be left in peace."

"My name is Josie Miller. I've just moved into flat six." Josie held out her hand.

The woman kept one arm locked across her chest, and with the second led a cigarette to her mouth for short angry puffs. "This is a respectable house. Or it used to be, until they refurbished and let the riffraff in."

"I assure you, I'm respectable, Mrs..." When the harridan did not supply a name, Josie said, "I'm a PA secretary at Lloyds TSB Bank, and the letting agent has my references. I'm sorry to bother you, but there are herring gulls by my window."

"In case you haven't noticed, this is the coast. Gulls live here."

"I'm just wondering how to treat them. I know they're a protected species..."

"Pests, that's what they are," the woman snapped. "Vile vermin, so don't feed them. Now excuse me. It's nine o'clock, and decent people have a right to peace."

The door clicked shut.

Josie checked her watch: eight forty-five.

#

She had to build a barrier. If she had furniture, she would push it in front of the window, and if she had tools, she would nail her blanket across. She managed to stand a suitcase on the inner windowsill, balancing her rucksack on top of it, filling the gaps with her still-wet towel and her winter coat.

Unless she held her hand very still, the pain was burrowing through her flesh. Holding the sponge for stencilling would be difficult tomorrow.

At least she no longer had to see the gulls. She lay on the carpeted floor, wrapped in her blanket, fantasising about a four-poster bed hung with drapes of rose-pink satin.

Klackedeklack. Scraaatch.

She turned on her CD player to drown out the seagull sounds. Thada-thada-doum-thad. The steady beat gave an excuse to her racing heart.

From below came outraged banging. The neighbour disapproved of the music. Josie plugged her ears with the ipod, but for once, the audio recording of Pride and Prejudice failed to absorb her. The fear in her stomach kept rising to her chest and throat, and she lay awake for a long, long time.

#

On waking, Josie's head ached and her throat scratched with thirst. She groped for the familiar lamp switch, and found only rough carpeted floor. Ah, yes, the new flat, and St Leonards, and the new job which had come up so suddenly.

Her brain felt like it had been boil-washed and tumble-dried. She stretched her aching limbs, scrambled up and stumbled to the window to pull the curtains back and let the dawn light in. No curtains, just a suitcase. Now she remembered: Seagulls.

When she undid the knotted hankie, she found the wound already healed over, the only slight discomfort coming from the tightness of the encrusted skin.

She lifted the suitcase away from the window.

Sunlight bathed the room. Outside, cool dawn changed into a golden morning, and the distant sea sparkled like diamond-sprinkled satin. Nobody had ever been killed by a wild bird. A breath of the fresh, salt-laden morning air would drive the last of the childish scares from her over-tired head.

On the other side of the road, three white-feathered, silver-winged gulls sat squatting on chimney-pots, haloed by the morning sun, a picture of romantic innocence.

Josie turned the squeaking handle and threw the window wide open.

They rose, fluttered, soared...and then they were upon her.

Rayne Hall writes fantasy, horror and non-fiction. Her black cat Sulu — adopted from the rescue shelter — likes to snuggle between her arms while she writes, purring happily.

After living in Germany, China, Mongolia and Nepal, Rayne has settled in a seaside town in England. She enjoys reading, gardening and long walks along the seashore, braving ferocious seagulls and British rain.

She is the author of over sixty books, mostly dark fantasy and creepy horror, as well as the bestselling Writer's Craft series.

Visit her website raynehall.com, or follow her on Twitter https://twitter.com/RayneHall for writing tips and photos of her cu

Cats and Dogs On Call
By Carole Ann Moleti

A night on call in a New York City emergency room is never easy. Interspecies cooperation is essential to everyone's survival. Most of the cool cats and down and dirty dogs have learned how to stick together when the moon is full and the poop hits the sidewalks, but Sasha is a very different breed.

Sasha always tests my obedience training. Siamese cats are an elite breed. Not like us sturdy pit bull mutts, steeped in tolerance for all species.

I dread an entire night on call with her. Sure enough, here she comes with her insulated lunch box—with a matching pink re-usable ice pack. I struggle to control my horror when she unzips and pulls out sardines for a quick nibble.

"Sasha, save some for later." I'm desperate for fresh air, and the shift hasn't even started. "It's going to be a long night."

"Yes, it is." She rolls her eyes, brushes off her whiskers with the back of her paw, and grooms the nape of her neck. Savoring the torture, she waits until the primping is complete to zip her lunch box back up.

Once the air clears, I unwrap my overstuffed, rare roast beef sandwich and dig in to what will probably be the last meal I get for the night.

"Smells like road kill." Sasha, still preening, peers at me through those narrow blue slits.

She opens her locker and pulls out a pair of ironed pink scrubs. Most of us change in the bathroom, given that any gender, genus or species could walk in at any moment. Not Sasha. She likes to show off and slithers out of her miniskirt.

A thong? For a night on call? Being so damn skinny, I guess she doesn't chafe like us stockier gals. Now that I've lost my appetite, I hide in the bathroom to change clothes so she doesn't notice the sensible white cotton briefs under my full figure, wrinkled institutional greens.

Out to get me for sure, Sasha still hasn't gone out to get ready for the shift turnover report. "It still stinks in here." She fans the air like it's my food that smells like fish three days past its expiration date.

"I guess cats and dogs have different tastes," I say, wondering if she's referring to my dinner or to me.

"Well, blue eyes and subtle tips on your ears distinguish Siamese from common felines. Our breed values exquisite gray highlights in our fur, and a svelte form." Sasha storms out of the locker room with her pink, diamond studded stethoscope collar, like she was the next cover girl for *Cat Fancier* magazine.

I'd like to dock her tail and bob her ears.

#

It's busy, not an empty crate or kennel to be found. I work my cropped butt off patrolling the perimeter. And I have seniority. "Can you please see the kitten in Bay 8 complaining of a cough?"

"Probably just fur balls. I'm too old to work this hard." She bookmarks the page of beauty secrets and dietary advice but doesn't move.

Maybe cats age faster than dogs, but she certainly hasn't lost any brain cells or reaction time. As soon as the Top Cat and Big Dog come sniffing around to see what's going on, Sasha springs into action and looks like she's been at it all night.

I go back to triage. Sasha makes sure to come tell me the outcome, nose and tail both skyward. "It was a fur ball, and it's his own fault. I'm going to the bathroom."

That damn cat spends more time scratching in perfumed dust than any of us dogs. I feel like howling at the full moon but maintain my professional comportment.

The ambulances roll in. It appears the streets have been emptied of strays, bloodied by a big gang fight, and dumped on our doorstep.

"I need some help out here, Sasha." Tired, hungry and very pissed, I bang on the door.

"I need more than three minutes every eight hours for a bathroom break. I will not be disturbed in my toilette by heathens, unschooled in proper etiquette and the social graces." She finally opens the door and sashays past me into the holding area.

I take a quick dump and get back to work.

#

We handle the mess, and I limp to the on call room.

It may be a community bunk bed arrangement, but it's a place to crash. Sasha has already ensconced herself on the bottom bunk, furthest from the phone, and pads it with that frilly, kitty crap. Then she pulls on an eye mask and inserts ear plugs.

Tom Cat, the ginger tiger anesthesiologist, shakes his head and curls up on the other end of the bed for a quick nap before they call him for the next case.

He's already been bitten one too many times tumbling around with Sasha in a basket of yarn balls, so he's done playing with her.

I scramble up to the top bunk and fall asleep despite the German Shepherd snoring under me. He gets a page and rushes off to the ICU. Someone bangs on the door to rouse the rest of us puppies and kittens for the next wave flooding the ER.

The waiting room looks like the scene of an animal rescue train wreck. Sasha is the only one still asleep, and I practically have to drag her out of bed.

"I have to brush my teeth, then I'll be along." She yawns and licks her whiskers.

"Why the hell did you go into hospital work?" I imagine I'm muzzled so I don't shake her until that thong rides up her scrawny, pink butt.

"My father wanted me to give something back, in thanksgiving for my family's superior genetic and aristocratic fortunes." She heads for the bathroom again.

I grab her tail but don't bite—yet. "I think you're part alley cat and just won't admit it."

Sasha spins around, and I dodge a pitiful swat from her front paws. She gets away, but rips off a nail and yowls.

I let her go—this time.

A low growl rises in the back of my throat and my ears flatten against my skull. I imagine grey fur scattered all over and pieces of feline dangling from the florescent light fixtures. Muscles tight, I'm ready to spring. It takes three long breaths before the red clears from my sight and I get back in control.

Sasha puts her skinny tail up and looks over that bony butt at me with narrow, ice blue eyes and that turned up nose, too perfect to be natural. "You wouldn't dare do that again."

Instinct overrules my conditioning. She's going to learn the lesson anyone who has had their tail docked and ears bobbed found out the hard way.

Teeth bared, I lunge after a warning shot. "Watch your ass, princess!

Carole Ann Moleti is a nurse practitioner in New York City, thus explaining her love of urban fantasy and everything paranormal. Her short stories have been published in the Mocha Memoirs Press and Ten Tales Series Anthologies. The third book in Carole's Unfinished Business series of paranormal romances is due out in 2017. Her award-winning non-fiction ranges from the sweet and sentimental to the edgy and irreverent. Visit http://caroleannmoleti.com for social media and links to her fiction and https://caroleannmoleti.info/ for nonfiction.

Bruised and Battered Nevermore
By Amy Grech

A dead man returns to avenge his murder.

Something strange about the decrepit apartment in Brooklyn where Jackie Crawford lived unnerved her. The lack of heat or hot water didn't set her on edge. Neither did the building's dilapidated condition evident from filthy hallways and the numerous cracks in the walls. No, it was something more ominous...

Her boyfriend, Jeff Dutton, pinpointed it one night while they snuggled on the couch and watched The Exorcist.

She leaned on his chest and he wrapped his strong arms around her to keep her warm, both inside and out.

When the movie ended, they heard a loud click that caused Jackie to flinch and set Jeff on edge.

"What was that noise?" Cringing, Jackie clung to Jeff.

"Beats me." He shrugged. "Maybe your creepy neighbor Al snuck in while we were watching the movie to poke around your lingerie drawer." Jeff snickered. "He looks like a pervert to me."

Jackie punched his arm, a playful love-tap. "That's not funny."

He stopped laughing. "Lighten up."

She curled up on the couch, too scared to budge. "Something's wrong. Go see what it is."

"Sure thing." Jeff got up to look around, straining to see in the dark. He flicked the light switch and searched for intruders. There was no one in the living room besides Jackie. For that he was grateful.

Cautiously, he made his way into the bedroom with Jackie following close behind, and turned on the light. They found the room unoccupied, but the window was open halfway despite the chill.

"Why did you open the window?" he asked, teeth chattering as he shut it.

She frowned. "I didn't. I thought you did."

"Nope, I didn't touch it." Jeff shook his head.

"I probably opened it last night to get some fresh air and forgot to close it." Jackie bit her lip, unable to remember touching the window.

"Why would you do that? It's a bit nippy out this time of year." He folded his arms and rubbed them to keep warm.

She scratched her head. "Why don't you go back into the living room while I whip up some hot chocolate."

"Sounds good to me." Jeff made himself comfortable on the couch while Jackie puttered around in the kitchen.

Five minutes later, she appeared holding two mugs of hot chocolate and set them down on the cluttered coffee table crammed full of books about ghosts and a collection of Poe's short stories.

"This is guaranteed to warm you up." Jackie smiled and handed a mug to Jeff.

"Not like you do." He kissed her deeply, making her blush.

She took a sip of her hot chocolate.

Jeff hoisted his mug and took a long drink. "Halloween's right around the corner."

"Should I be scared?" Jackie rested her head on his shoulder.

"Yeah. I think you've got ghosts." He leered at her.

She laughed. "What gives you that idea?"

"You've got a window that opened all by itself and, seeing as how you don't remember doing it what else could it be?" Jeff set his empty mug in his lap.

Jackie finished her hot chocolate and went into the kitchen. "I don't know. That noise we heard could have been anything."

"Like what?" He followed her.

Her eyes lit up. "A stray cat knocking over a garbage pail."

"It sounded much worse than that. Didn't it?" Jeff put his mug in the sink.

She nodded. "Let's go see if Sy is home. Maybe he can get to the bottom of this."

"Who's Sy?" He leaned against the wall.

Jackie gave him a dirty look. "The Super, remember?"

Jeff opened his mouth to speak, but Jackie cut him off before he could get a word in edgewise.

"If we know why the spirit is unhappy, we can hold a séance to help undo the wrong, and hopefully put an end to these strange happenings." She bit her lip.

"What's with all this spirit mumbo-jumbo? I didn't know you were into that." Jeff frowned.

"You don't believe in ghosts, do you?" Jackie grabbed her keys off the kitchen table.

"Not unless I can see them. You know, like Casper the Friendly Ghost?" He wiggled his fingers in the air for effect.

"There are no 'friendly' ghosts. Besides, Casper the Friendly Ghost is a cartoon character." She pointed to numerous books about the subject scattered on the coffee table.

He slammed the door shut and followed her to the Super's apartment on the first floor. "How would you know?" Jeff frowned.

"I just do." She gave him a dirty look. "You wouldn't understand."

He shrugged.

They walked down three flights of sagging stairs to Sy's apartment.

Jackie knocked once and waited. As, usual, Sy Mann had the TV blaring, so she knew he was home.

They heard him shuffle over to the door and fumble with three locks. "Don't get your panties in a knot. I'm comin'," Mr. Mann's stern voice declared.

Jackie cleared her throat and blushed, caught off guard by the old man's choice of words. Jeff snickered.

The door creaked open and Sy Mann a tall, slight man with fluffy tufts of white hair sticking up every which way appeared in the doorway. Mr. Mann smiled when he saw Jackie but looked confused when he realized she wasn't alone.

"Hello, Jackie. I had a feeling it was you." He grinned revealing toothless gums and waved.

"Really?" Jackie winked.

"Oh, just a hunch. Who's that young fella?" He pointed a trembling finger at Jeff.

She sighed, embarrassed that he forgot so soon. "This is my boyfriend, Jeff. I introduced you to him a few weeks ago."

Jeff extended a hand and Sy shook it.

"Ah, of course. Now I remember. He looks like a fine young man." Sy scratched his head, looking confused. He opened the door wide and led them inside.

Jackie and Jeff stepped carefully to avoid slipping on the worn linoleum and old newspapers with yellow stains strewn about.

"You're wondering why my hands shake, aren't you, boy? I saw you staring." Mr. Mann glared at Jeff.

He nodded slowly, dreaded the answer.

"My nerves are shot, but you don't want to hear about that—it's an awful story for another time." Sy shook his head.

Jeff admired his own strong, steady hands. "Fair enough."

Mr. Mann petted the ancient orange tabby with rheumy, green eyes sprawled out next to him on the unmade bed. He sat on the edge and motioned for Jackie and Jeff to take a seat. They sat on the rickety, wooden chairs that faced the bed and creaked under their weight.

"What can I do for you?" He scratched Tiger's chin.

Jackie leaned forward so Mr. Mann could hear her clearly. "Do you remember why the last tenant who lived in my apartment moved?"

"What?" Sy frowned, eyeing Jeff suspiciously.

Tiger purred, too content to realize the conversation did not match his mood.

Jeff sighed. "The tenant who lived in the apartment before Jackie moved in. What happened to him? Did he commit suicide, or did he die of natural causes?"

"The guy who used to live in Jackie's apartment? Let's see..." His eyes lit up, full of recognition. "Oh, sure, I remember Marty Leary; odd fellow. Always came and went at weird hours, usually in the dead of night. Never did figure out what he did for a living. I just know the rent was always paid on time. That's all the landlord really cared about." He scratched his head. "Why do you want to know how he died?"

"Strange things have been happening in my apartment lately." Jackie sat forward and bit her lip.

Sy rubbed his pointy chin. "Like what?"

Jeff folded his arms. "Yeah, strange noises and windows opening by themselves."

"Sounds like you've got a spook. Maybe even a couple of 'em." Mr. Mann chuckled.

"I think knowing how the last tenant died might help solve the problem." Jackie took Jeff's hand in hers and squeezed.

Sy studied Jackie. "Let's see...Give me a minute. He'd been dead for a couple of weeks last summer when the tenants complained about the terrible stench coming from the place; smelled just like rotten meat, they said. So I dug up the spare key I had for 4-D and went to investigate. I found poor Marty in bed, rotting; his blue eyes glazed over and wide with fright. The covers pulled up to his chin, and his rigid fingers curled up into claws." Mr. Mann pulled a cat treat out of his shirt pocket and fed it to Tiger. "The coroner removed the body late at night, so the chances of someone seeing were less likely. According to the autopsy, a heart attack did him in. But from the look on his face, I'd say he was scared to death by someone he didn't expect to see, and that's what killed him!"

Deep in thought, Jeff shuddered. "So much for your theory, Jackie." He glared at her.

"What theory would that be?" Sy shifted his weight on the bed.

She lowered her head, feeling dejected. "I told Jeff if we contacted the spirit of the deceased we could find out what made it unhappy, we could correct the problem so the strange occurrences would stop and the spirt could find peace."

"How long have these 'strange occurrences' been going on?" Sy frowned.

Tiger made himself comfortable on Mr. Mann's lap, and settled down for a nap.

Jackie crossed her legs. "Over a month now."

"I see. Is it unusually cold in your apartment?"

"Yeah, why?" Jeff folded his arms. "I think the radiator's busted."

Sy's green eyes twinkled. "No, it isn't the radiator— the spirit's presence is making your apartment so cold. I can prove it."

Jeff stood and started to pace. "I've heard just about enough of this nonsense! If you're so sure it's Mr. Leary's ghost, show us how to drive it out."

"Don't show anger, or try to chase it. That will only make things worse. Take it from someone who knows...." Mr. Mann stroked Tiger.

He rolled his eyes. "How do you chase a ghost? You can't see it..."

"There are ways son, but I don't think you'd understand." Sy stared at Jeff.

Jackie sat forward in her chair. "I suggested holding a séance."

"That might just do the trick." Sy nodded.

She breathed a sigh of relief. "Would you do the honors, Sy?"

"Why me?" He set a frail hand on his chest.

Jackie smiled, putting him at ease. "You knew the dearly departed."

"Not very well I'm afraid," Sy shook his head.

She leaned back in her chair, feeling more relaxed. "But you were on good terms with him, weren't you? A familiar voice might help draw out his spirt."

"Oh, I suppose. It's worth a try." Mr. Mann stared at Jackie, taking her questions seriously.

"I'll bet he had an unresolved gripe; that might explain why his ghost lingers in Jackie's apartment, looking for closure. Isn't that right?" Jeff smirked, feeling smug.

"Could be, but I think Marty wants revenge." Sy grinned.

Tiger twitched in his sleep, dreaming of big, black birds.

"Will you help us?" Jackie clasped her hands together, practically begging.

Gingerly, Mr. Mann lifted Tiger up and set him down on the bed. "You betcha." He got to his feet slowly, with a little help from Jackie.

She smiled, obviously relieved. "You have no idea how much I appreciate this."

"Yeah, things that go bump in the night are downright scary when they aren't on the big screen." Jeff shivered.

She led them back to her apartment. On the way out, Mr. Mann grabbed a white pillar candle and a book of matches.

When they got upstairs Jackie unlocked the door and switched on the light. "Jeff, go check see if the heat is on while Mr. Mann prepares the kitchen table."

"No problem." When he walked over to the radiator under the open window and cautiously reached out to touch it, hot metal scalded his hand. Jeff screamed, ran into the kitchen and grabbed some ice cubes from the freezer to soothe his throbbing fingers.

Sy winked. "I told you the heater wasn't broken. Now do you believe me?"

"I do now!" Jeff licked his swollen fingers.

Jackie rushed him over to the sink and ran cold water over the burn. "Oh my God, Jeff! Are you alright?!"

"No, my hand is killing me." He pressed a cold, damp cloth over his swollen hand.

Mr. Mann placed a plate under the candle and lit it in the middle of the kitchen table and shut off the light, bathing them in its eerie glow. "Both of you sit down. It's time."

Jackie and Jeff reluctantly followed.

"Now, take my hands. Bow your heads and be quiet." He took a deep breath before he began.

They each took a wrinkled, liver-spotted hand, focused on the candle's flickering flame and waited.

"Marty, if you're here, give us a sign. This is Sy Mann, the superintendent of the building you died in. I need to ask you a very important question." He cased the room.

A minute later all the books in the bookcase near the kitchen came tumbling down. Jeff cringed. "Maybe this wasn't such a good idea after all."

"It's too late to stop now." Sy winked.

Startled, Jackie tried to bolt from the table, but Jeff held her down.

The dictionary landed at Sy's feet. He leaned over for a closer look. Coincidentally, it opened to the M's; a minute later, a raven flew into the room and landed between the pages, it's beady black eyes twinkled knowingly.

Mr. Mann addressed the bird. "Marty, tell us how you died."

In answer, the raven rested its beak on the word murder for a moment and pecked a hole in the page.

"Do you know who killed you? Caw twice for yes, once for no."

They all looked on in awe as the raven cocked its head to one side, as if to ponder the question for a moment before cawing twice.

Sy smiled expectantly.

Jackie and Jeff gawked at the raven, unable to believe their luck. They leaned in for a better look at the mysterious messenger.

Mr. Mann followed his hunch. "Did Al Ash kill you?"

The raven cawed twice more and flapped its wings.

"Do you know why?" Sy smiled.

This time, a single caw was the reply.

"Will you rest in peace if we get Al to confess?"

The raven cawed twice more before flying off.

The candle went out, casting them in darkness.

#

Al Ash lived on the fourth floor, in the apartment directly across from Jackie; the climb seemed to take forever, since Mr. Mann had to stop several times to catch his breath.

Jeff whispered in Jackie's ear: "I can feel myself growing older."

"Shut up, Jeff." She jabbed him in the ribs. "You'll be old too, someday."

He gritted his teeth. "Not if I can help it."

Jackie gave him a dirty look.

When they reached the top, Sy knocked on the door and waited.

A gruff voice answered: "Who is it?!"

"Sy. Can I come in?" He smiled broadly.

"Why? Is there a problem?"

"Could be. Open up so we can talk."

He peered through the peephole. "Who's that with you?" Al cracked the door for a closer look. "I don't like the looks of them!"

"Jackie and Jeff. She lives in Marty Leary's old apartment. Jeff's her boyfriend."

"What do they want? They aren't cops, are they?" Al ogled his uninvited guests.

Sy shook his head. "They just want to ask you some questions about Marty's death. Some strange things have been happening in the apartment lately and they're trying to find out why."

"So, is that my fault?" He laid a hand on his chest.

"Maybe." Mr. Mann wedged his foot in the doorjamb, before Al slammed it shut. "Maybe not. It depends."

Reluctantly, Al undid two locks and opened the door.

He stepped aside and they went in. Unlike Sy's place, this apartment was immaculate not a speck of dust anywhere. Copies of The New York Times and The Rifle Rack were stacked on the antique coffee table in date order, and from the glimpse they caught of the bedroom, they noticed a bedspread pulled so taut you could bounce a quarter off it.

Sy sat between Jackie and Jeff on the couch. Al made himself comfortable in his worn recliner and stretched his long legs.

Mr. Mann clasped his hands together so tightly his knuckles turned white. "Al, why did you kill Marty?"

Al laced his fingers and rested them in back of his head. "Why I should tell you?"

Sy pointed an accusing finger at Al. "If you confess, I promise you'll be much happier. I don't think you know how miserable all this guilt has made you. Admit it, it's eating you up inside."

He gnashed his teeth for a few minutes before answering. "All right. He stole my wife! Are you happy now?" When he spoke, his voice was icily calm.

Jackie's jaw dropped. "You're kidding."

"Could you be more specific?" Jeff frowned.

"Are you people stupid?! He had an affair with her! When I caught them in bed together, I just snapped—I wanted to end it, quick and dirty. Plenty of muss, no fuss." Al rubbed his sweaty palms together and glared at his firing squad.

Sy shook his head. A raven flew into the room and landed on his bony shoulder to listen in. "Al, when I found Marty's body he was in bed alone. Your wife was nowhere to be seen. And there were no signs of forced entry. How do you explain that?" His green eyes locked on Al's pale, blue ones.

Al nodded slowly and finally broke down: "I found a spare key to his apartment under her pillow while I made the bed one morning. When I saw that I went berserk. I rushed over to Marty's place, slipped the key into the lock, and stepped inside. I found my wife wriggling around beneath him and told her to get out of my sight while the getting was good. She struggled to break free from Marty's grip, scooped her clothes up off the floor, and hightailed it out of there before I could get my hands on her. It's a good thing, too, because there's no telling what I would've done." He rubbed his bloodshot eyes and stopped to collect his thoughts.

"When Marty saw me coming with my hands balled up into fists, he pulled the sheets up to his nose and seemed to be bracing himself for the worst beating of his life. Just when I was getting ready to strangle him, I bent over, half expecting him to beg for forgiveness, but he didn't say a word, even though his mouth was wide open. I thought he'd be screaming or trying to run away, so I leaned in close to his face to see if he was breathing. Imagine my frustration when I checked his wrist for a pulse and discovered he was already dead."

Sy shook his head. "You sound disappointed, Al."

"I am! I wanted to ring his scrawny neck!" Al did a double take when he saw the raven perched on Mr. Mann's shoulder. "How'd that damn raven get in here?"

"Maybe you left a window open." Jeff snickered.

Jackie nodded. "You never know who might drop in, especially in New York."

"Sy, what the hell are they talking about?" His eyes locked on the raven and he spat on the bird.

He scratched his head. "Al, that raven has something important to tell you."

The raven cawed twice in agreement.

Al stood up and walked over to Sy for a closer look. "I hate ravens, they're evil!"

"That's Marty Leary's ghost, Al. His spirit has been lingering in my apartment ever since the day you scared the life out of him. He's got a score to settle with you." Jackie stared at Al, eyes full of contempt.

"Give me a break, that's no ghost! It's just a damn bird!" He reached out to grab the raven and missed. "Prove that's Marty's ghost."

In response the raven swooped down and let something shiny slip from its sharp talons. The object landed on Al's lap with distinct click! He picked it up and stared; it was a key with Apt. 4-D written on a scrap of paper taped to the top.

"That's pretty wild!" Jeff grinned.

Jackie patted Mr. Mann on the back. "Nice work."

"Boy, that Marty sure is clever! I have a feeling he's just getting warmed up." Sy's eyes twinkled.

Al let the key dangle between slender fingers. "4-D. Isn't that where Marty lived?"

Mr. Mann clapped his hands softly. "Congratulations! You won the grand prize!"

"What am I supposed to do with this damn key?" Al waved it in the air.

Jackie shook her head. "You'd better think fast; the raven is headed straight for you."

"Turn around or you'll miss it!" Jeff pointed to the black bird.

Al shifted his gaze at the exact moment the raven made a beeline for his face. He swatted blindly when the raven plucked his eyes out swiftly, and devoured them. Still clutching the key, overturning the coffee table while crimson tears flowed freely from the new holes in his dense head, Al shrieked and stumbled, scattering the neat piles of magazines and newspapers everywhere.

Sy smiled, happy to see a wrong righted at last.

Jackie screamed and buried her face in her hands, shocked by the raven's gruesome act.

Unable to tear his eyes away, Jeff looked on, lost in morbid fascination.

Al's massive hands continued to grab and swipe, missing the crafty raven by a mile; it landed on his broad shoulder and pecked his meaty neck with its pointy beak, going for the jugular. He howled as his hand found his attacker, seizing the raven in a death grip and squeezing, until all the life flowed out of the brave, black bird.

Bruised and battered...nevermore.

Amy Grech has sold over 100 stories to various anthologies and magazines including: *Apex Magazine, Beat to a Pulp: Hardboiled, Dead Harvest, Detectives of the Fantastic, Volume II, Expiration Date, Fear on Demand, Fright Mare, Funeral Party 2, Inhuman Magazine, Needle Magazine, Reel Dark, Shrieks and Shivers from the Horror Zine, Space & Time, Tales from The Lake Vol. 3, The Horror Within, Under the Bed,* and many others. New Pulp Press recently published her book of noir stories, *Rage and Redemption in Alphabet City.*

She has a story forthcoming in *Creepy Campfire Quarterly.* Amy is an Active Member of the Horror Writers Association who lives in Brooklyn. Visit her website: http://www.crimsonscreams.com. Follow Amy on Twitter: http://twitter.com/amy_grech

Pookie Has Two Daddies
By April Grey

Things get complicated for this cunning canine.

"Hey Pookie, Daddy's going away on another business trip, and I'm leaving you with Mommy down the hall."

Pookie, a black and white, long-haired Chihuahua, wagged his tail frantically and whined at the door. As soon as Jeff opened it, Pookie raced down the hallway of their small apartment complex.

"Why Pookie? You're ready to stay with us?" Giving Jeff a friendly wave as he walked down the stairs with his luggage, Alice closed the door. She scooped up Pookie in her ample arms and he licked her face. "Look who's with us, Albert!"

Albert looked up from his newspaper and grunted. "Tell him to leave some dog food for the mutt next time. How long?"

"Just a few days."

Mommy was Pookie's favorite person in the whole world, second to Daddy of course. She let him sit on her lap all day, stroking and grooming him. And she always cooked him fresh chicken breast and as well as the leftovers from their meals. But he missed Jeff something awful. If only Mommy and Daddy would

131

live together! But Mommy lived with Not-The-Daddy Albert, and Daddy lived alone.

If only…

"Albert, Pookie needs his walkies, but if I leave the fish on the stove it'll burn."

"Okay. Okay." Albert grabbed the leash off the doorknob. "Don't want to have to clean up any messes."

Pookie yipped his approval and skipped to the door. A brilliant solution to his problem came to mind.

#

"Oh, Jeff, how nice of you to come." Alice red-eyed, with trembling lips gave her neighbor a hug.

Jeff blinked away a tear. "Not at all, I feel terrible about this happening. I'm glad I was home in time for the funeral. What was it I heard—that he fell while taking Pookie for a walk?"

"Yes, on the stairwell. You know Albert's eyesight hadn't been too good of late."

He held the old woman at arm's length, searching her eyes for forgiveness. "I feel responsible."

"Not at all, and Pookie has been such a comfort in the past few days." Her face lit up as she turned to the tall, handsome man by Jeff's side. "Oh, and who is this?"

A huge grin plastered itself on Jeff's face as he patted the arm of the man beside him. "This is George. We met in San Francisco on my last business trip. He's moving in with me."

April Grey is the editor for *Hell's Garden: Mad, Bad and Ghostly Gardeners* and *Hell's Grannies: Kickass Tales of the Crone*. Under her married name she also edited twenty novels for Damnation Books. Her short stories have appeared in many venues and are collected in: *The Fairy Cake Bake Shoppe* as well as *I'll Love You Forever*. She is the author of two urban fantasy novels: *Chasing The Trickster* and its sequel, *St. Nick's Favor*. Her dark fantasy, *Finding Perdita*, will be published by Caliburn Press soon.

http://www.aprilgrey.blogspot.com
author.to/aprilgrey
www.aprilgrey.com
twitter @aprilgreynyc
https://www.facebook.com/april.grey.5

Mad About Pigeons
By Yurika S. Grant

A retired mad scientist living in the British countryside plots the downfall of all pigeon kind. He soon learns that some dogs are best left sleeping…

In a large manor house deep in the British countryside, a voice rose in anger.

"Bloody pigeons!"

"Woo-woo, wu! Woo-woo, wu!" came a friendly response from just outside an open window on the second storey.

Again, the vexatious voice was raised in agitated annoyance.

"Where is my damn shotgun, Sebastian?"

"I believe it was lodged in the rear end of a ring dove, last I saw it, sah," replied a second voice, one that could only belong to a butler, elderly and expressive.

On the second of three storeys, threadbare brown curtains billowed in and out as they were blown by a gentle autumn breeze, wafting hints of pine and rose and maybe just a minor indication of bovine flatulence into one of many bedrooms. In the room, a man; mid-thirties with hair as dark as milk-free coffee, shaggy and unkempt.

The colour brown featured heavily. Brown shirt, brown trousers, brown blazer, brown shoes, brown room.

135

A veritable symphony of earthen excitement. Next to him, a rather older man in a butlering outfit of white and black held a shotgun, almost reverentially so, polishing and cleaning it of pigeon remains acquired after a wholly enjoyable time thinning the flock last evening.

"Ah, yes, ring dove. An appropriate name for where I shoved the shotgun, is it not, Sebastian?" said the brown man. "One might say I doved it where the sun doth not shine, hah!"

"As you say, sah," the butler Sebastian said, his tone carefully neutral.

Sebastian's lord and master, one Algernon Octavius Crumplethwait the Third, had always been a handful, ever since his younger years when he would experiment on insects and small rodents to see what made them tick. Thirty years on and he was more or less the same man; it was simply the scale of his experiments and the length of his temper that had changed.

Sebastian handed the sparkling shotgun to his lord. "All clean, sah."

Algernon accepted the weapon, muttering in a mildly murderous fashion as he loaded two shells. "Pigeons… contemptible birds. Good-for-nothing little bas—"

"I believe collared doves are the blighters that make all the hullabaloo, sah."

"Spare me your semantics, Sebastian." Algernon strode to the window, located the source of his annoyance – perched on the window ledge and peering at him with beady eyes – and pointed his shotgun with malice aforethought. The next sound was a brief 'woo-woo-boom!' and a cloud of feathers. "That'll learn the little stinker, hah!"

"I'll get the brush."

"And bring me the Righteous Boomstick of Pigeon Perturbation while you're at it, this little pop gun won't do at all. I need to blow off some steam."

"Followed by blowing off some bobbing heads, sah?" Sebastian asked, moving over to a large walnut cabinet and opening it, revealing several rifles, a number of shotguns, and the aforementioned boomstick.

"Quite so, yes." A brief jaunt outside once Sebastian had cleaned up the mess, and Algernon was ready for a spot of clay pigeon shooting in his gargantuan mansion's grounds.

Much like its owner's appearance, the mansion's garden had an unkempt and untidy look with creepers creeping, plants protruding through the pavings, and hedges hedging their bets.

Algernon grumbled. "Need to do something about the pigeon problem, that much is certain. Being up all night with my experiments in the basement, I simply cannot have the little bar studs keeping me awake all morning with their incessant cooing."

Algernon enjoyed clay pigeon shooting a great deal. He found it most therapeutic vis-à-vis his pigeon-related woes. Almost as enjoyable as whack-a-pigeon, in fact.

A few minutes were duly spent setting up, then...

A heavy 'thunk!' punctuated the still morning air, trailed by a Doppler-shifted 'woo-woo, wu!', which was in turn followed by an ear-bending 'boom!' and several dozen feathers spiralling to the ground. Algernon preferred to use live pigeons.

"An excellent shot, sah, if I may be so bold as to observe," Sebastian said, setting another portly pigeon into the machine.

"Thank you, Sebastian. I find the report of a throaty boomstick quite alleviates the stresses of modern life."

As an oft-retired mad scientist, one of Algernon's earliest and most-beloved inventions had been this very boomstick, a blunderbuss firing high quality lead buckshot. At least, it originally fired lead buckshot. These days he had to make do with inferior metals.

He loaded a fresh batch of bismuth-tin shot. "In my day, we used real lead shot! These days, they're all, 'oh you can't use lead shot, that's poisonous and harmful to birds'. Poppycock!"

"Indeed, sah, one wonders exactly how much more deadly to birds it is possible to get than exploding them into a cloud of feathers."

"And that is why you are my butler, Sebastian, you fully understand the plight of a retired mad scientist whose only crime in life was to revive the dinosaurs and send them rampaging down Pall Mall. I don't know what all the fuss was about. I think the whole thing was blown entirely out of proportion."

"I personally have never seen the Queen looking quite that cross before, sah."

"Yes, I believe I may have ruined my chances for a Knighthood, there. Load up another pigeon, old boy, I feel the stresses of modern life returning with gusto."

"Very good, sah." Sebastian did so, releasing another Doppler pigeon into the wild blue yonder, where it was promptly turned into a bright red mist.

Reloading, Algernon continued muttering. "Enjoyable though this is, I wonder if we could speed up the process? Maybe a second barrel? Or incendiary shot? I could always tie two—"

"Perhaps explosive bullets might be helpful, sah? With homing capabilities like that movie you watched once? Or maybe some Claymores set with pigeon feed and proximity sensors?"

"Homing explosive bullets... yes, that is a good idea. Remind me to make a few of those."

"Would sah like me to remind sah before sah embarks on sah's work in the basement, sah?"

Hefting his boomstick, Algernon gave his butler a vague wave of a hand. "If you would, old boy, you know how I forget things when I'm working. Pigeons won't kill themselves, after all. I can't be slacking off in my important research."

"And would sah enjoy his usual Pigeon Mess for supper?"

"No, I believe I shall have the Dove Delight tonight, if it's all the same to you."

"I shall prepare one later." Sebastian loaded three pigeons and launched them skyward.

"Oh, the old three birds, one boomstick manoeuvre? Challenge accepted!" Algernon said in a gleeful tone. "I will have some peace and quiet around here!" he yelled at the expanding cloud of feathers, post-fire.

"Wonderfully ironic, sah, if you don't mind my saying."

"Yes, it was, wasn't it? Now, I believe I shall spend the rest of the morning attempting to sleep. Then it'll be a delicious Dove Delight followed by an evening of discovering the best ways to disintegrate pigeons. Life is good."

Late that afternoon, with a steaming hot dove pie bubbling away in the range, Sebastian made his way upstairs to his lord's room. The pigeon-shaped alarm clock — battered, cracked, and scuffed from its frequent flights across the room — had just gone off, filling the room with the dulcet tones of bloody pigeons.

Algernon had once been asked why he used the noise made by his number one nemesis as his alarm clock's tone. His response was thus; because no bloody way could he sleep through that thrice-accursed racket of spittle-inducing awfulness.

Stretching, he sat up in the enormous four-poster he called his bed. He swung his legs out to find his favourite slippers — old faithful as he affectionately thought of them — and sniffed a few times. "Ah, what a delightful scent to wake up to. I can almost taste the salty tears of pigeonkind as I savour one of their own, cooked to perfection."

Sebastian held out a bath robe. "Perhaps you could use their delicious tears as a condiment, sah?"

"Yes… yes, indeed. I wonder if it might be possible to squeeze the liquid out of one? A pigeon pepper grinder of sorts."

"Worth a try, sah?"

Algernon nodded a few times as he tied the robe. "To the garden!" Outside, standing comfortably in his robe and slippers, he carefully sighted along the barrel of a dart gun loaded with tranquilisers. "Steady… steady…"

A 'pff!' sound accompanied the dart exiting the barrel, followed by a distant 'coo-gerk!' as a pigeon dropped out of one of the many trees dotting the landscape and thudded softly onto the grass.

Sebastian checked his pocket watch. "Just in time for dinner, sah."

A tantalisingly tasty dish of delectably delightful dove stuffed with roast vegetables and drizzled in wine and spices was enhanced ever so slightly by the addition of sweet avian tears.

Algernon enjoyed his supper at the kitchen table, a mahogany affair older than he was, and eventually sat back with a satisfied expression. "Mm, exactly what the doctor ordered. And since I am the doctor, I know what I'm talking about!"

"We have that delivery of pumpkins coming tomorrow, remember, sah," Sebastian said as he quickly and carefully tidied the crockery away.

"Halloween, by Jove! Best time of the year and no mistake. Always enjoyed a spot of mulled wine and a slice of pumpkin pie as a little whippersnapper. It's just not the same without Crumplethwait Senior, but we make do. Do we not, Sebastian?"

Pausing in the act of washing up in the cavernous sink, Sebastian stared blankly at the cracked and peeling plaster of the kitchen wall. "Quite so, sah. Most unfortunate, being trampled by elephants in the Serengeti, but he did manage to take quite a number of them with him, I recall. Never one to roll over and surrender, old Lord Crumplethwait the Second."

"Dynamite up the trunk, hah! The old bastard never missed a trick. Right up until he did." Algernon snorted a pinch of snuff in as regal a fashion as he could manage, and placed his feet up on the table. "Still, his servants were well fed for the next several weeks. Elephant meat is quite filling, or so I hear."

"Made a fine piano, too, sah," Sebastian added as he got back to his tasks.

"That, they did, once they retrieved the bits and pieces and put them back together." Algernon dropped his legs back down, wandered to one of the cupboards, and poured a glass of fine brandy. "Care to join me for a little tipple, old boy?"

Drying his hands on a towel, Sebastian sidled across and took a proffered glass. "Very good, sah. To Lord Crumplethwait the Second, may he rest in pieces."

"Cheers!" Algernon drained the glass in one go. "Righto. To work I go!"

After a meal as good as that, the perfect way to finish the evening off would be to spend it engaged in dastardly and devious experiments in his basement laboratory. Workbenches lined both the walls and centre of the dim space while glasses, tubes, pipes, and all manner of arcane odds and sods — as Algernon referred to the tools of his craft — covered every flat surface, and even a few of the vertical ones.

Never before had he faced an enemy such as pigeonkind. They bred like mad, crapped all over absolutely everything, and regularly woke him from pleasant dreams. And while he enjoyed a spot of sport involving shotguns and explosives, those methods simply weren't practical for large-scale extermination.

Around six the next morning, Algernon finally crawled into bed after a productive evening in the lab. Unfortunately…

"Woo-woo-wu! Woo-woo-wu!"

"Sebastian!"

"Right here, sah."

Crawling groggily back out of bed, Algernon pointed to one of his many wardrobes. "Fetch me my Lab Coat of Scientific Significance. Enjoyable as blowing the little blighters up can be, I believe it's time for a more dramatic solution to our problems. I believe I have the very thing."

"Ah, time for an all-dayer, sah?"

"'tis the only way, if I'm to get any blasted sleep."

Dressed in his usual brown ensemble with a white lab coat over the top, they ended up in the laboratory where Sebastian immediately noticed something new and interesting.

"Might I enquire as to the purpose of the vats of green bubbly stuff, sah?"

"My latest triumph: liquid death!" Algernon said with gleeful malevolence.

"Liquid pigeon death, I assume, sah?"

"And possibly many other things. The virus is, after all, untested."

Sebastian rolled up his sleeves and sat at an ancient PC with a crackling and buzzing CRT screen. "Ready when you are, sah."

"Jolly good! First, delivery method."

"Aerosol seems wise, sah."

"Exactly my thoughts!"

The clacking of stiff, yellowed keys echoed back and forth like the rattle of Death's teeth as Sebastian entered some details.

"I'm using the same formulas and equipment as that delightful batch of Kill-o-Matic-3000 you invented several years back, sah. Is that acceptable?"

Algernon's eyes sparkled. "Ah, the old Kill-o-Matic Bug Destroyer. One of my better inventions and no mistake."

"Verily, the locusts did not know what hit them, sah. Quite the altruistic invention for once, sah."

"Even mad scientists have occasional changes of heart."

Sebastian sat back. "Liquid Death has been vaporised. Transferring to pressurised containers for dispersal." He tapped another button. "Ready, sah."

Algernon paced. Back and forth, back and forth, fidgeting and idly rubbing a thumb over an old silver pendant left to him by Crumplethwait Senior. "Soon, Sebastian. Soon, I shall have my peace and quiet!"

"A master work in dedication and vindictiveness, sah," Sebastian said, clearly admiring.

Algernon stopped his pacing. "Truly, pigeons are the Devil's familiars."

"I meant you, sah. Also, isn't that cats, sah?"

"No... no, I don't believe that for a second, old chap. Cats are delightfully vicious creatures when they feel like it, playing with their food and all that. I feel something of a kinship with them."

"Very good, sah. Shall I let slip the gasses of war, sah?"

"Yes, let the little blighters have it!"

Sebastian did as requested, releasing the aerosolised virus into the atmosphere and watching the screen with eagle eyes, alert for any changes.

Sensors placed around the country allowed for near-instantaneous data on any and all relevant experiments, a convenient holdover from the last time Algernon had decided he despised a particular animal.

Sebastian noted some worrying data in addition to the expected pigeon casualties. "The virus has mutated and jumped species, sah."

"That was fast. Remarkably so."

"It appears the virus is making use of the high speed trans-optic vein network to propagate further and faster, sah," Sebastian muttered.

"From my old Faster Than Night experiment? How devious of it."

"Perhaps we should have dismantled the network, sah."

"Balderdash! Old experiments are a perfect springboard for new experiments. Which species has it jumped to, incidentally?"

"Humans, sah."

"Well, some losses are to be expected in any great endeavour."

"I am not entirely certain that seven million can really be considered 'some', sah."

"Spare me your moralising, Sebastian. The pigeons are being equally decimated, are they not?"

"Quite so, sah."

"Then the experiment is a success. Quit your bellyaching."

"Very good, sah." Sebastian peered at the screen. "Oh dear..."

"Another problem?" Algernon asked, exasperated.

"Depends how you define the word, sah," Sebastian replied, scanning the screen in hopes that he had merely read the data wrong.

"Out with it, man!"

"At the currently rate of mutation, humanity will be the second most dominant species on Earth approximately one week, sah. The pigeons are evolving, sah. Rapidly, sah. Sorry, sah."

"Oh."

"Truly, they are like the cockroaches of the avian world, sah."

A gentle sigh escaped Algernon's lips. "They are at that, Sebastian, you are quite correct."

"Perhaps sah should have bought a pair of earplugs, sah?"

Another sigh. "What would I do without you, Sebastian?"

Ten years and one week later…

Algernon Fluffywing the First crawled into bed after a tiring but wholly enjoyable day spent thinning the herd. His beaked head nodded and bobbed as his butler tucked him in. "That was a splendid Ascension Day celebration and no mistake! Much better than that silly old Halloween nonsense."

His butler nodded, an involuntary reflex brought about by the pigeon genes. "Quite so, sah. Shame about all the hullabaloo, sah."

"Bloody humans! I shall have to do something about them one of these days."

A bout of chattering floated through the open window into the mansion's bedroom, emanating from the general direction of Algernon's human farm.

He sighed. "Fetch me my Boomstick, would you, old boy?"

Outside, he sighted along the barrel of his Righteous Boomstick of Human Harassment as his butler set up for a spot of clay pigeon shooting, a silver pendant hanging loosely around his ruffled neck. A heavy 'thunk!' punctuated the still night air, followed by a Doppler-shifted and familiar voice yelling, 'What did I do to deserve this…!'

Algernon preferred to use live humans.

Yurika S. Grant: Living in the rain-soaked flatlands of Lincolnshire in the East of England, Yurika spends most of her time writing, with occasional breaks to engage in normal person activities such as eating and sleeping. But only occasionally.

If you enjoyed the works of these wonderful writers, please do use the links to let them know or leave a review at your retailer.

Other Works by April Grey

Aging is not for the faint-hearted, yet there is little choice in the matter. You can take good care of your health, your finances, your loved ones and still life will throw a curve ball. In this anthology you will find tales of courage, of women who rise to the challenges of time in many different ways. Ten talented authors give their take on the theme of Grannies from Hell. Edited by April Grey.

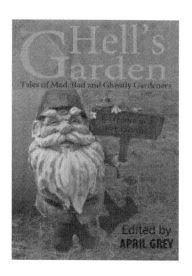

Six talented writers explore the various paths Evil can take when in Hell's Garden. Featuring tales by Rayne Hall, Heather Holland Wheaton, Jonathan Broughton, Mark Cassell, Eric Dimbleby and Jeff Hargett. Edited by April Grey.

Sexbots threaten to destroy a marriage. A half-alien embryo remains the only hope for the human race. Tempting cupcakes that aren't just bad for your waistline, but may result in permanent injury. Welcome to the realm of April Grey. Steampunk Zombies, The HG Avenger, Nefarious Chihuahuas, Lothario Dolphins, and many other bizarre characters lurk in these short stories.

What is love? In the eye of the beholder or something more? In these four dark tales, zombies, ghosts, ancient spells and modern crooks show us that love conquers all—even death and despair. Includes I'll Love You Forever, The Vision, and stories from Troll Bridge.

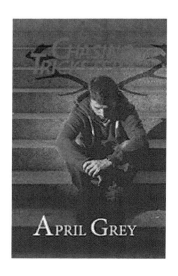

One Man, Two Women, Two Gods...who will survive the Trickster's snare? Ghostly images materialize in Nina Weaver's photos. Goons try to kidnap her. When her photographs are stolen and her best friend is shot, she realizes that she has no one to turn to but her ex-lover, Pascal "Goofy" Guzman. Together they go on a desperate road trip in search of answers. The truth is darker and more terrifying than Nina could ever have imagined. After their love re-ignites, they fall into the Trickster God's trap.

St. Nicholas asks Nina Weaver to be his emissary. Her mission is to take a one-way trip five years into her past to save the lives of thousands of children. Doing this will result in her losing the life she has built in New York City, including her relationship with Pascal Guzman. Nina faces down corporate greed, attempts on her life and the terrors of the Trickster God to keep her promise.

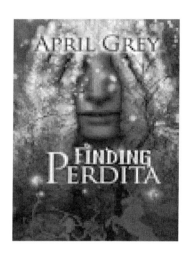

Down on her luck and out-of-work, actress Cindy White's life changes—and not for the better—when her roommate kicks her out. Landing in new digs in an old Chelsea tenement Cindy discovers a tunnel from the building's basement that leads to the land of Perdita, a place she'd thought her father had made up in the fairy tales he'd once told her.

A dangerous, ruined place of fairies, demons and captives—like her father, whom she thought was dead.

In Finding Perdita, a dark fantasy, a young woman discovers her true self and must align it with the old, leaving the world she knows behind in an effort to free her father.

19242848R00092

Printed in Great Britain
by Amazon